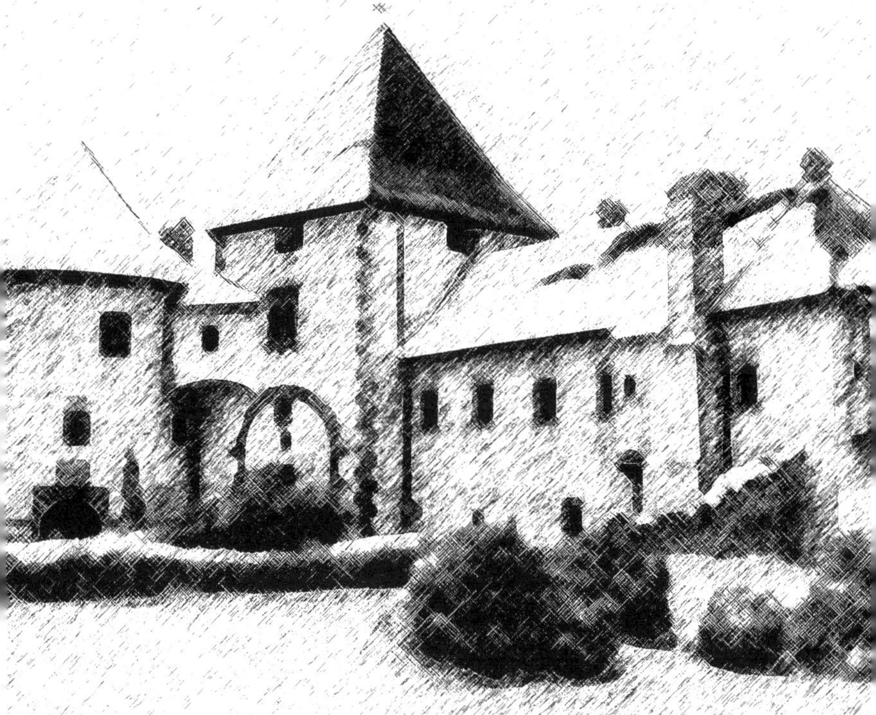

CHRISTMAS AT THORNCLIFF MANOR
SECRETS AT THORNCLIFF MANOR, THE SERIES

Copyright © 2017 by Sophie Barnes

All rights reserved. Except for use in any review, the reproduction or utilization of this work in whole or in part in any form by any electronic, mechanical or other means, now known or hereinafter invented, including xerography, photocopying and recording, or in any information storage or retrieval system, is forbidden without the written permission of the publisher.

This is a work of fiction. Names, characters, places and incidents are either the product of the author's imagination or are used fictitiously, and any resemblance to actual persons, living or dead, business establishments, events or locales is entirely coincidental.

Printed in the USA.

Cover Design and Interior Format
© THE KILLION GROUP INC.

CHRISTMAS AT THORNCLIFF MANOR

SECRETS AT THORNCLIFF MANOR

THE SERIES

SOPHIE BARNES

BY SOPHIE BARNES

Novels
Christmas at Thorncliff Manor
A Most Unlikely Duke
His Scandalous Kiss
The Earl's Complete Surrender
Lady Sarah's Sinful Desires
The Danger in Tempting an Earl
The Scandal in Kissing an Heir
The Trouble with Being a Duke
The Secret Life of Lady Lucinda
There's Something About Lady Mary
Lady Alexandra's Excellent Adventure
How Miss Rutherford Got Her Groove Back

Novellas
The Duke Who Came To Town
The Earl Who Loved Her
The Governess Who Captured His Heart
Mistletoe Magic (from Five Golden Rings: A Christmas Collection)

To all the readers who have loved escaping to Thorncliff Manor, this is for you.

CHAPTER ONE

England, 1820.

COMFORTABLY SEATED AT A DINING room table that seemed to stretch toward infinity, Fiona Heartly considered the people who'd been invited to visit Thorncliff Manor during the holidays. Due to the group's intimate size, only a fraction of the table had been set for the evening, while most of the chairs remained eerily empty. Pleasantly, however, five large oranges pricked with cloves and strategically placed in the center of the table infused the air with a seasonal fragrance of citrus and spice. The lady of the manor, the Dowager Countess of Duncaster, looked as formidable as ever. Placed at the head of the table, she wore an elaborate wig that had long since gone out of fashion. But she was known to have several eccentric bones in her body, so nobody ever minded. Rather, Fiona suspected she was considered all the more interesting on account of her peculiarities.

To Lady Duncaster's right sat the Duke of Lamont, a middle-aged gentleman whose demeanor was always perfectly somber. Fiona had yet to see him smile, but then again, she had also to spend more than one minute in conversation with him. A long-time friend of Lady Duncaster's, the pair had apparently been spending the holidays together for almost six years now. Ever since the duke inherited his title with the sudden passing of both his father and brother.

Leaning forward, Fiona glanced toward the seat at Lady Duncaster's left. Lamont's cousin Viscount Belgrave sat there, amicable as usual. He'd always struck her as being exceptionally kind and good natured, though not the sort of man who would ever stir an amorous interest in her. She needed someone more challenging – a scoundrel with a good heart. Not that she had any intention of marrying any time soon. As the youngest of her siblings, she knew she still had a year or two ahead of her before seeking a husband became a necessity. In the meantime, she meant to enjoy what remained of her independence – the final moments of her youth.

That particular thought had her looking directly across the table at one of her favorite people, the Earl of Chadwick. He'd always humored her hoydenish streak, and he never failed to enjoy a bit of mischief as much as she did. He'd been a part of her family for as long as she could remember – ever since her brother Christopher, Viscount Spencer, or Kip as his family called him, had brought the earl home with him for a visit one year during the school holidays. They were all exceedingly fond of Chadwick. His positive outlook on life was so infectious it was impossible to be grumpy while keeping his company.

Meeting Fiona's gaze, he smiled warmly. A couple of seconds elapsed, and then he suddenly snatched up his napkin and started dressing his fork as if it were a lady putting on an extravagant ball gown. Fiona's lips quirked, more so when the fork began dancing along the edge of the table.

"Oh," Lady Duncaster said, "How utterly delightful!"

Had they been anywhere else, his behavior would have been considered incredibly improper. But here nobody minded. Rather, they all appeared quite entranced by Chadwick's little performance, which now included a softly hummed tune as his knife swept in to partner with the fork in a waltz.

"I suppose it's no wonder you are so good at charades and other parlor games," Rachel observed. "Playing pretend comes so naturally to you, I almost envy your ability." Exceptionally fond of mathematics and science, she rarely found anything amusing since all jokes were usually ruined for her on account of their nonsensical facts. But with Chadwick, she often made an exception. It seemed he had a style that appealed to pretty much everyone.

"Speaking of which," Lady Duncaster said, taking a sip of her wine, "I would like to discuss our holiday schedule. Montsmouth has yet to arrive of course, but I see no reason why we cannot agree on a few diversions without his presence."

Fiona instantly frowned. She vaguely recalled seeing the Earl of Montsmouth when she'd last visited Thorncliff during the summer, but he'd always lingered in the background, so she hadn't paid him much mind. It never would have occurred to her that he might be a good enough friend of Lady Duncaster's for her to include him in this private holiday gathering. No doubt he'd been delayed on account of the weather.

When she'd arrived that afternoon with her parents and her sisters Emily, Laura, and Rachel, snow had already begun to fall. Her other siblings, Christopher, Chloe, and Richard, had chosen to spend Christmas at their individual estates with their spouses, no doubt so they could have the privacy newly wedded bliss required. Not that Fiona minded since her brothers' absences, in particular, would allow her to move about Thorncliff more freely and to continue her search for the treasure she still believed to be hidden there.

It hadn't been found yet, but certain clues had, like a diamond earring linked to her own family, a code book outlining a conspiracy within the aristocracy, and a letter tying her great-aunt to the late Earl of Duncaster's father and to some sort of strange resistance movement that had been active during the time of the French Revolution.

"Is he the gentleman who lost his snuff box in the conservatory this summer?" Laura asked, still speaking of Montsmouth.

"Yes," Fiona's father said.

"I find he's always standing on the outside of things," Lady Duncaster added, "and with both parents dead and no siblings to speak of, I thought he might like some company for Christmas."

"How good of you to take such notice," Fiona's mother said, smiling.

Lady Duncaster chuckled. "Oh, I am always taking notice." She glanced at each of them in turn, her lips curling into a secretive smile that made Fiona suspect they weren't here by chance but that Lady Duncaster had taken particular care in selecting each of her guests. The lady regarded them each with her piercing blue eyes and then quietly asked, "How about skating for a diversion?"

The question came so suddenly, Laura looked as though she might choke on her wine. "Right now?" A touch of alarm tightened her words.

"Don't be absurd," Lady Duncaster admonished. Stabbing at her food, she selected a piece of meat and popped it into her mouth.

Fiona decided to return her attention to her own plate. She didn't quite manage it, though, before catching a glimpse of Chadwick, who was now making odd expressions with his eyes. Biting her lip, she forced back a laugh and shook her head. His pout only made him look all the more ridiculous. Honestly, he could be such a child sometimes.

"I am simply trying to determine which activities you might enjoy while you're here," Lady Duncaster continued. "Since the lake is solidly frozen, it might be fun for all of you to go for a spin on it."

"I would love to," Laura said. She'd always been good at skating. Much better than Fiona, at any rate.

Lamont frowned. "I see no need to risk a broken limb."

"It sounds as though you might have had a bad experience once," Laura said with compassion. He paused for a moment before saying, "I simply wish to be careful."

Laura stared at him briefly and then quietly nodded. "I understand."

This seemed to surprise him. "You do?"

"Of course. I fell from a tree once and broke my ankle. It took forever before I chose to go climbing again."

"At least a year," Fiona said. She recalled the incident well enough, since she'd been up in the tree as well when the blasted branch had snapped beneath her sister's weight.

"That was quick," Lamont remarked.

Laura shrugged. "I realized watching my brothers and sisters enjoy the activity was worse than any fear I had of falling again."

"Still," Lamont murmured, "I think I'd prefer to watch the skating rather than participate in it myself."

"Have you ever actually tried it?" Laura asked.

A look of discomfort crossed the duke's face. He sipped his wine and then turned toward Lady Duncaster. "How about a sleigh ride?" he asked, avoiding Laura's question. "Might that be possible?"

"As long as we get enough snow," Lady Duncaster said. She smiled openly at everyone. "We should also try to find a yule log soon and make some more decorations. There are pine trees and pinecones out in the woods, and the ladies will probably enjoy shopping for ribbons in the village."

"If we gather the pine before going to town, we'll be able to estimate the exact length of ribbon we need for making garlands," Rachel said. She glanced about the room, her gaze assessing.

"What a practical suggestion," Belgrave murmured.

"I see no reason not to strive for efficiency when one is able to do so," Rachel said, arching a brow. The expression made her look more like a critical matron than a marriageable young lady.

Fiona almost groaned. She'd tried to advise her sister many times before on her hair styling, clothing, and social skills, but Rachel refused to let anything but practicality and fact guide her. It made Fiona wonder if her sister knew what it meant to have fun — a thought that saddened her since having fun was so vital to her own existence.

She glanced across at Chadwick once more, unable to stop herself from smiling as she watched him tell Laura a joke. Perhaps the two would develop a *tendre* for each other during the next couple of weeks and eventually marry. It was something Fiona had considered more than once after noticing how animated her sister became when keeping Chadwick's company. It would certainly be wonderful to finally make him a definite part of the family.

"So now that your three oldest children are settled, Lady Oakland," Lady Duncaster said, "one cannot help but wonder who might be heading for the altar next."

"Not me," Rachel said with immediate swiftness. She glanced around before explaining, "I've more important matters to see to than courtship."

"All you need is to meet the right gentleman," Laura told her dreamily. Having embarked on her second romantic novel, she loved the idea of happy endings and forever afters.

"As I've pointed out before, statistics have proven it is unlikely he even exists. And if he does, he is undoubtedly so far removed from my little part of the world, meeting him would prove rather improbable."

"Good lord, Rachel," Laura huffed. "Matters of the heart cannot be reduced to numbers and equations. You'll see when love strikes you. It will happen when you least expect it and probably with a man you would never have considered."

"That is how it happened for your mother and me," Lord Oakland said. He directed a wink and a smile at his wife.

"*I* was supposed to marry my husband's friend through an arranged marriage," Lady Duncaster put in. "He escorted me back to England from India, though, and we fell in love during the voyage."

"And look at Spencer, Chloe, and Richard. None of them came here looking for romance," Lady Oakland pointed out.

"I will admit, Richard has surprised me," Rachel said. After he had lived in seclusion for five years, nobody had expected him to marry, let alone find an opportunity to meet a wife. And yet, against all odds, his wife, Mary, had captured his heart.

"It only goes to show there is hope for all of you," their father said. "Even you, Rachel, despite your obvious resistance to the issue."

"Very well," she agreed. "Find me a man who will enjoy conducting scientific experiments with his wife and who would be proud of her publishing mathematical theories, and I might consider falling for him."

"Hear, hear," Fiona said. She'd decided to support her sister in this, for if there was one thing she truly believed in, it was finding commonality in a relationship. Without it, such a relationship would surely flounder.

Leaning forward a little, Belgrave gave Rachel a curious look. "If I might ask, what sort of experiments are you working on exactly?"

Rachel froze. Her lips parted, and it occurred to Fiona this might be the first time anyone outside the family had bothered to show an interest in her sister's work. Rachel blinked twice, set down her fork as if doing so would help her regain her composure, and finally said, "Presently, I'm following Sir Humphrey Davy's instructions on how to make an electric arc."

The silence that followed was palpable, until Belgrave eventually said, "As I understand it, you will need to build a battery in order to accomplish such a goal."

"Yes. I am aware," Rachel said, her focus on the earl more intense now than it had been before. "I've purchased most of the items I require, but I am still waiting for the oil of vitriol to arrive. It should have arrived by the time I return home from here."

"I thought your focus was mainly on," Lady Oakland waved one hand as if the air would provide the answer, "the movement of slugs, as I recall."

Fiona groaned and as she did so, she saw Chadwick conceal a smile. He leaned forward, narrowing the space between them as much as possible. "Parents can be so ignorant sometimes when it comes to their children."

"I wonder what they imagined might have been in all of those boxes Rachel's been purchasing recently," Fiona whispered back.

"Slugs, from the sounds of it."

Doing her best to stop from laughing resulted in a loud, indelicate snort. Fiona pressed her hand over her mouth in time to catch a look of disapproval in her father's eyes. He frowned and shook his head, silently warning her to behave. She glanced back at Chadwick, whose expression had transformed into one of pure, innocent ignorance.

"I'll get you later," she mouthed.

He merely shrugged.

"—something for me to do while away for the summer," Rachel was saying. "But it's hardly going to get me a fellowship at the Royal Society."

"The Royal Society?" Lord Oakland stared at his daughter. "That is quite ambitious of you since I don't believe they admit women."

"Someone has to be the first," Rachel told him, as if the society's exclusion of the female sex was only a minor inconvenience.

"I completely agree with you there," Lady Duncaster said, "but you will likely have to make an impressive contribution of your own to even be considered. Copying someone else's experiment is hardly going to suffice."

"I know," Rachel said. She set her napkin beside her plate. "Recreating the arc is only the beginning. What I plan to do is invent an electrical lamp."

Another moment of silence descended on the room while everyone tried to process this bit of information. Fiona smiled in Rachel's direction. Her sister might own a rigid personality, but she loved how easily she'd stunned her family and friends this evening.

"Do you think anyone would want to use such a thing?" Emily asked. "It sounds as though you're making it more complicated for people to get light into their homes, rather than simplifying the issue. Striking a flint is such an easy task, but batteries with oil of vitriol and whatever else might be required…nobody will want to bother with that, surely."

"Perhaps not," Rachel said. "The only way to know is to try."

Fiona glanced around the table and wondered what the rest of the dinner party might be thinking – if they saw how imaginative Rachel truly was. Her ability to envision the need for a new invention and her intention to try and create it were nothing short of impressive. It made Fiona wish she had such a purpose in life, something besides being a proper lady and marrying well. Recalling the Thorncliff treasure, she determined more than ever to find it over the course of the next two weeks. Doing so would be an incredible victory for her family since it would, hopefully, see her great-aunt's jewelry returned.

"You may adjourn to the library for your after-dinner drinks, if you like," Lady Duncaster told the gentlemen when they eventually rose from the table. "The ladies and I will take our tea in the music room in case you wish to join us there later."

Fiona followed the group out into the hallway, her thoughts on her upcoming treasure hunt. She could scarcely wait to retire for the evening so she could set her mind more fully to the task. Perhaps if she—

The touch of a hand against her arm made her

flinch, and she instinctively turned to find Chadwick walking beside her. His eyes met hers with a spark of amusement, and the edge of his mouth kicked up to form his signature smile. "I don't believe I've told you how fetching you look this evening, Fiona."

"You don't look half bad yourself," she replied, offering him the typical sort of rejoinder that had set the tone for their relationship over the years.

He linked his arm more fully with hers, bringing them closer until their shoulders touched. "I've missed you, you know."

His voice was warm, his breath even warmer as it brushed along the side of her neck, producing a spark in the pit of her belly – a sudden awareness that had never existed before.

Unnerved by it, she tugged her arm away from his. "Yes." *Good lord*. Why on earth did she sound so breathless?

Confused, she crossed her arms, hugging herself as they walked and effectively preventing further physical contact. Hesitantly, she glanced up at him, only to be met by a pair of inquisitive eyes – eyes that seemed to be filled not only with Chadwick's usual good humor but with something else as well…something she could not quite define.

"We've missed you too," she told him hastily. "A pity Kip and Richard won't be joining us. I'm sure you would have liked to see them."

"Of course." A touch of humor trembled upon his lips, and for some absurd reason, it made her feel more uncomfortable than she'd ever felt before in his company. It was almost as if he knew a secret he'd chosen to keep from her, one that might see her made the subject of some wild and ridiculous joke. "But," he added in a hushed whisper as he suddenly turned quite serious, "I was actually more interested in seeing you."

And since they'd arrived at the music room, he did not linger to elaborate on his cryptic comment, but strode off, following the rest of the gentlemen to the library. Fiona stared after him, unable to comprehend the sudden tightening of her stomach or the pattering of her heart. He was like a brother – a dear friend and partner in mischief. Except she felt as though something between them had changed in the last second, and it bothered her to no end that she couldn't quite figure out what that something might be.

CHAPTER TWO

EDWARD ROTHBURN, EARL OF CHADWICK, followed the other men into the library.

"What will it be?" Lord Oakland asked. He was studying the selection of carafes in the library. "Brandy, port, or claret?"

"Brandy for me," Lamont said, going to assist the earl.

The rest of the group concurred with that choice while laying claim to a nearby seating arrangement. Given the massive size of the Thorncliff library, there were several of these throughout, allowing for private reading or conversation corners during the warmer months of the year when Lady Duncaster turned her home into a guesthouse. The estate had rapidly received a fabulous reputation. It had become the place in which one wished to be seen. Being so confirmed a certain level of income because Thorncliff was no cheap holiday retreat.

Taking a seat in a deep leather armchair, Edward thanked Lamont for the brandy set before him. "A toast," he said, once everyone else had a glass in hand, "to a happy Christmas spent amongst friends." He took a sip of his drink, enjoying the warmth of the amber liquid as it slid down his throat. It was good to be back here again with the Heartlys, for he had not seen them since the summer, deliberately keeping his distance until he was sure of both heart and mind.

"So tell me, Chadwick," Lord Oakland said. He set his glass aside and gave him a welcoming smile that conveyed deep interest. "What have you been doing for the last four months? We kept expecting you to come and call on us like you always do, but instead, you've stayed away."

He'd known this question would come, so he was ready with his answer. "My estate was in dire need of attention. The storms in October damaged many of my tenants' homes and flooded one of the fields. I decided it was best to stay and oversee the work in need of being done, instead of relying on my caretaker alone."

"Don't you trust the man?" Lamont asked.

"Certainly, but the land and the property are my responsibility. It felt wrong to abandon all the hard work while I went away to visit with friends."

"You share my way of thinking," Belgrave mused. "I have always believed in setting a good example for my men by lending a helping hand. Built a wall last spring, and found it mightily rewarding." Setting his glass to his lips, the viscount downed a fair portion of his brandy.

"I saw the benefits of such thinking when I was in the army," Lamont said. His remark provoked a moment of silence while everyone recalled the tragic events that had brought him home early. His father, brother, and sister-in-law had all perished simultaneously during a carriage accident, leaving

Lamont the new duke and making him the sole guardian of his two young nieces. He'd brought the girls with him to Thorncliff, and although Lady Duncaster had invited them to join the adults for dinner, the girls had favored the nursery she had prepared for their arrival. "At Waterloo, there was no such thing as being too good for the work that had to be done, though I did see a few aristocrats snubbing their noses at the prospect of digging latrines. They failed to gain the same degree of respect as those who chose to forget about titles."

"There's nothing like war to bring out the best and worst in all men," Lord Oakland muttered. "My son Richard can attest to that."

"He's an honorable man," Lamont said. "My only regret was leaving him to carry out the scouting mission that got him captured. I was supposed to go in his stead and would have done, had I not been called home."

"You mustn't blame yourself. You had your duties to attend to, and with no heir of your own, risking your life in war was no longer an option."

"Thank you." Lamont's expression remained severe. "I appreciate your understanding, my lord, considering all your son had to go through before he escaped and managed to return."

Edward quietly pondered that statement. Everyone had believed Richard was dead these past five years. He'd been stunned to discover Kip's younger brother was still alive and living in hiding. "I'm glad to see him happy," he said.

"Mary has had a miraculous effect on him," Lord Oakland agreed. "I'd begun thinking he would never recover from his ordeal, but she has been like a saving angel for him. The entire family owes her a tremendous debt of gratitude."

"One often hears people complain about marriage and all of its disadvantages," Belgrave said, "but in Richard's case, it seems to have come as a blessing."

Lord Oakland snorted. "Those who claim they wish to avoid it are ignorant fools."

"You only have the liberty to say so because your own marriage is such a success," Edward teased.

"Nonsense." Lord Oakland brushed his comment aside with the swipe of his hand. "An unmarried lady cannot take lovers without scandal, while an unmarried man will continue to take on mistresses or worse, thus risking any number of ailments. Both have needs that must be met. Once married, they may satisfy each other to their heart's content."

Edward almost choked on his brandy. "What an astute observation."

Belgrave chuckled, while Lamont grew rather flushed. The subject matter did not seem to agree with the duke in the least.

"I see no reason to mince words," Lord Oakland said. "After all, we are all grown men here and friends to boot. I've known the three of you most of your lives, have even held you when you were a babe, Belgrave. Your mother was horrified when you spit up all over my new jacket. And you, Lamont. Have you forgotten that I helped your father convince you to overcome your fear of horses? We've history, gentlemen. Enough for me to speak plainly when in your presence."

Edward knew he was right. Still, he couldn't help

but wonder if the earl might maintain such views if he knew how he felt about Fiona – the real reason behind his prolonged absence.

"Given your frame of mind regarding marriage," Belgrave was saying, "you must be exceedingly pleased to have settled two sons and one daughter as quickly as you have."

Lord Oakland nodded. "Oh, indeed. It makes me wonder how long it will take to settle the rest."

"Lady Duncaster seems to be of the opinion one or more will form an attachment during the next two weeks."

"Which would suggest that one of you gentlemen must be prepared to make an offer." Lord Oakland regarded them each in turn, his gaze as assessing as any judge's. "My daughters are exceptional women. They deserve all the happiness in the world, and as much as I respect you gentlemen, I am not entirely convinced any of you are ready to turn your backs on your bachelorhoods." He downed the remainder of his drink and stood. "If you will please excuse me, I do believe there's a matter I'd like to discuss with my wife. I trust you'll join us in the music room when you are ready?"

Edward watched him go, while carelessly drumming his fingers against the armrest. "He doesn't think we're deserving of his daughters."

"What father does?" Belgrave asked.

"I do believe there are many who can be easily convinced by the depth of a man's pockets," Edward said.

Belgrave chuckled. "How right you are, Chadwick."

"I must confess," Lamont said, drawing attention,

"my decision to spend Christmas here again this year hinged heavily on Lady Duncaster's assurance that Lady Laura would be in attendance."

"You have an interest in her?" Edward asked, suddenly intrigued. He wouldn't have thought a man so serious might be drawn to a woman of such genteel sweetness. Then again, why on earth wouldn't he be?

Lamont expelled a deep breath and frowned. "My nieces require a mother figure – a lady to teach them proper manners and comportment. I have no idea how to manage it myself, and their governess, as talented as she is, can only do so much for them."

"So you intend to seek Lady Laura's hand for practical purposes alone?" Edward asked. "I'm sure Lord Oakland will be thrilled with the news."

"She would gain a formidable title," Lamont insisted.

"Indeed she would," Edward agreed. He gave the duke a candid stare. "But the lady herself is a romance author. Do you honestly believe she would marry for anything less than love?"

That brought a pensive frown to the duke's forehead. "I must confess, I hadn't considered it. My interest in her is based mostly on my appreciation for her character."

"I rather like Lady Rachel myself," Belgrave said, and then hastily added, "if I *had* to choose, that is."

Edward reached for his drink. "As I recall, you developed a *tendre* for Richard's wife, Mary, when we were last here." He set the glass to his lips and drank.

"Only until I discovered her affections lay elsewhere." Belgrave held up his hands. "I would never try to bend someone's heart to my will or steal another man's love interest."

"The carefreeness with which you speak suggests *your* heart was never fully engaged, or you would not have surrendered so easily in your pursuit of her," Lamont pointed out.

"You are correct," Belgrave said, dipping his head. "I found her to be delightful, but I cannot claim to have ever loved her."

"But you believe you might grow to love Lady Rachel?" Edward couldn't quite figure it out. The two seemed so vastly different from each other, he with his *joi-de-vivre* attitude toward everything and she with an intellectual touch of severity. And yet, Belgrave's interest in Rachel's experiments at dinner did suggest they might have more in common than one would suspect.

Belgrave considered them each in turn. "If you must know, I find her fascinating. As for love, how can I be sure if I'll ever feel such depth of emotion for her unless she and I spend more time in each other's company?"

Edward stared at him for a second. "Are you planning to court her?"

"In a manner of speaking." The viscount turned suddenly serious. "I would greatly appreciate you not mentioning it to anyone."

"I shan't utter a word," Edward promised.

"Neither will I," Lamont added.

"So then," Belgrave said, after a brief moment of silence, "if I pursue Lady Rachel and Lamont here pursues Lady Laura—"

"I might have to reconsider my intentions, considering Chadwick's earlier remark about her expectations," Lamont said.

Belgrave paused as if this comment was worthy of great contemplation. Intent on changing the subject since he feared what Belgrave might say next, Edward was about to suggest they go and join the ladies when the viscount finally spoke.

"The truth of the matter is that as wonderful as it has been to remain unattached, we've all surpassed our thirtieth year. Perhaps it is time for us to stop keeping mistresses and see to our responsibilities instead."

"I have certainly waited long enough," Lamont said. Stretching out his legs, he seemed to fall into deep pensiveness.

"The point is, we have a unique opportunity here," Belgrave continued.

"And what would that be?" Edward asked, even though he suspected he already knew the answer.

"We have a chance to gain the favor of four lovely young ladies without any other gentlemen interfering." Belgrave met Edward's gaze with a sigh. "Granted, you've always had a close relationship to the Heartly daughters, but for the rest of us, I dare say we ought to make the most of our stay here."

"I quite agree," Lamont said without elaborating any further on his comment.

Edward felt his heart ricochet a little as he considered Belgrave's proposal. He had never confessed his growing affection for Fiona to anyone, not even her brother Spencer, whom he considered his closest friend. The fact was, the eleven years between them often made him wonder if he wasn't too old for her. He feared having such concerns confirmed by others or, worse, of being prevented from spending time with her if her parents decided to disapprove of his feelings. Now, faced with Belgrave's insightful words, he drew a deep breath.

"If you gentlemen wish to pursue Lady Rachel and Lady Laura in earnest, then I will promise to do my best in keeping my distance from them."

"What a good sport you are," Belgrave said, "and besides, I'm sure you would rather spend your time in Lady Fiona's company anyway."

Edward felt the skin prick at the nape of his neck. He forced himself to meet the viscount's gaze with a casual ease he did not feel. "What do you mean?"

Belgrave smiled. "It is common knowledge the two of you have always been close. She's like the little sister you never had, or something like that. Your exploits are infamous, Chadwick. Didn't you know?"

Edward shook his head. He'd never considered it.

They sat for a moment in silence, and then Belgrave said, "It's a pity Lady Emily shan't be receiving the same amount of attention as her sisters."

The door opened, and a man wearing in a green velvet jacket and a pair of brown trousers stepped in. Holding a silver tipped walking stick, he peered at them all through the monocle he held to one eye. "Good evening, gentlemen. I apologize for my delay."

"Montsmouth," Edward declared. He rose to greet the newly arrived earl. "What impeccable timing you have!" Turning toward Belgrave, he added with a mischievous smile, "I believe your concern has been put to rest." And with that promising remark, Edward went to join the rest of the party in the music room, leaving Belgrave and Lamont to tell Montsmouth he would have to give his attention to Lady Emily.

CHAPTER THREE

WHEN FIONA ENTERED THE DINING room for breakfast the following morning, she found only Rachel, Chadwick, and her parents present. "Is the rest of the party still sleeping?" she asked while she made her way toward a side table on which eggs, bacon, sausages, kippers, bread rolls, and a variety of jams had been set out.

"Lamont has gone for a ride," Chadwick said. Glancing in his direction, Fiona saw he was carefully watching her over the rim of his coffee cup. She averted her gaze and picked up a plate, unnerved by the strange flash of heat his perusal provoked. "I passed him in the hallway on my way here," he added while she selected her food.

"Emily and Laura have yet to make an appearance," Fiona's mother said, "and I recall Lady Duncaster being a late riser. As for Montsmouth and Belgrave, I really can't say."

Fiona crossed to the dining table and took a seat beside her father, putting her diagonally opposite Chadwick, who continued to watch her with a twinkle in his eyes. "What is it?" she asked, cutting her bacon.

Chadwick's expression was suddenly blank. "What do you mean?"

Pressing her lips together, Fiona stared across at him for a moment with the intention of conquering the strange sensations he'd stirred in her since the previous evening. It didn't seem to be working. For some peculiar reason, her stomach was doing the most disconcerting twist. *Ridiculous*. This was Chadwick, for heaven's sake. No reason for her to have a fit of nerves in his presence. Especially since she was not the sort of woman prone to jitters of any kind.

"You've been watching me since I walked in," she told him.

"Would you rather I ignore you?"

"No, of course not, but I—"

"Fiona," her father said, "let's not begin the day with an argument. Personally, I don't see where else he should have looked. You became the subject of attention the moment you said good morning."

Frowning, Fiona stabbed at her bacon, catching a piece and putting it in her mouth just in time to see Chadwick give her a victorious look that made her want to pull him out of his chair and throttle him. She paused, staring into the tea a footman had poured for her. Why was Chadwick making her so irritable today? It made no sense at all when the two of them had always enjoyed an easy sense of camaraderie. She loved his company, and yet she sensed something changing between them. It was a most unpleasant feeling.

"We should probably gather the pine today, don't you think?" Lady Oakland asked.

Rachel nodded. "Did Lady Duncaster say which

rooms she wished to decorate?"

"No."

"Then how are we supposed to estimate the amount of pine we'll need for the garlands?"

"As difficult as it may be for you," Lady Oakland told her daughter, "I would recommend simply gathering as much as we can carry and seeing how many decorations such quantities will provide."

"That sounds terribly inefficient," Rachel grumbled.

"But a great deal simpler," Fiona said, offering Rachel a sympathetic smile, "and perhaps a bit more fun."

"I find your proposal quite formidable, my dear," Lord Oakland said, addressing his wife. He sipped his coffee. "But you and I may have to leave the children to it. If you'll recall, we have another errand to attend to."

"We…oh…er…yes," Lady Oakland said, finishing off with a broad smile.

Fiona stared at her mother's befuddled expression. "What errand?"

"Well, Fiona, it is Christmas, you know. I'd say your mother and I are entitled to keep a few secrets from you."

"Quite right," Chadwick said, drawing Fiona's attention toward him once more. She saw he appeared to be doing his best to keep his expression as bland as possible. Still, she didn't miss the little twitch that pulled at the corner of his mouth. For whatever curious reason, the man was having a tremendous amount of fun. "I would be happy to escort Rachel and Fiona to the woods and help them carry the pine back to Thorncliff."

"That is extremely kind of you," Lady Oakland said.

"Although there's really no need," Fiona said. She caught her breath when her gaze snapped onto Chadwick's. Never in her life had she made a deliberate effort to avoid his company and yet now... "I'm sure there are servants who might assist so Chadwick may be spared the ordeal. Would you not prefer to stay here and play cards?"

"With whom?" he asked, the question so direct and assessing he forced her to avert her gaze. "Your parents will, by their own account, be busy as well; Rachel will go with you, Lamont is already out, and the rest of the guests are still sleeping."

"While I cannot speak for Belgrave, I'm sure Laura and Emily will be down soon," Fiona told him.

Folding his arms, Chadwick leveled her with a frank stare. "Am I mistaken, or are you deliberately trying to get rid of me?"

"I can't imagine she would do such a thing," Lady Oakland said with no small degree of surprise. "Fiona has always stuck to you like glue."

Sitting back, stiff as a fence post, Fiona did her best to maintain her composure. "Mama is right. Of course I'm not trying to get rid of you." She reached for her teacup and shrugged one shoulder before raising the delicate piece of china to her lips. "Don't be silly, Chadwick. You know I adore your company." What she hated was that she hadn't felt like herself since he'd whispered against her ear the previous evening.

"Excellent!" He pushed his chair back and stood. "Shall we meet in the foyer in say...half an hour?

I will see about acquiring some baskets for all the pine you ladies plan on collecting." With a wink directed at Fiona, he strode off while she stared after him, perturbed by the fact that she suddenly noticed how broad his shoulders appeared beneath the cut of his jacket.

"You don't seem yourself today," Rachel whispered. She and Fiona walked alongside each other with Chadwick following a short distance behind. The snow that had fallen the previous evening was thick enough for Fiona to feel her boots sinking into it with every step. It would allow Emily and Laura, who'd made their appearance a short while earlier, to take the sleigh out with Montsmouth if they wished. "If something is troubling you and you would like to discuss it, you know I'm always ready to lend an ear."

"Thank you, but I'm sure it's nothing." Linking her arm with her sister's, Fiona tried to offer her an explanation. "Perhaps I'm simply tired. You know how I can be when I don't get enough rest."

"Churlish?"

"Very." Grinning, Fiona was pleased to see Rachel was smiling, and so she dared say, "Lord Belgrave was rather attentive toward you last night. Tell me, what is your impression of him?"

Glancing sideways, Rachel looked out across the frozen lake they were passing. They turned onto a path that would take them past the Chinese pavilion and directly toward the forest. "He seems pleasant enough."

"He showed great interest in your experiments."

Although she kept her face averted, Fiona heard the note of pleasure in her sister's voice when she said, "So he did."

"Perhaps your statistical calculations are wrong, and there is a man worthy of your attention right here at Thorncliff."

Rachel's posture immediately stiffened. A lengthy moment of silence followed, and then, "I am not the sort of woman to inspire romantic musings. As pleasant as Belgrave may seem, I very much doubt his interest in speaking with me went beyond the academic."

"I fear you may be too harsh on yourself," Fiona murmured. "And I think the better question is whether or not you will be able to have a romantic interest in him."

"Fiona, I—"

"If you decide you do," Fiona continued without pause, "I will happily help you improve upon your appearance which, as you're aware, is rather drab. But if your own sister who loves you won't say so, then I cannot imagine who will."

"You know I have always valued your honesty, Fiona, but I would prefer it if a gentleman were to admire me for my mind rather than my looks."

"And he shall," Fiona assured her, "but that doesn't mean he doesn't deserve to see you at your best."

They reached the path leading into the forest, only to find it blocked by a fallen tree. "Might I offer assistance?" Chadwick asked, moving closer.

"How kind of you to notice we're in need of it," Rachel said. She allowed Chadwick to hold her hand for support while she stepped over the obstacle.

"You're next," Chadwick said and turned toward Fiona. There was warmth in his chocolate-colored eyes, but he did not smile this time when he held out his hand in quiet invitation. Rather, he appeared uncharacteristically serious and, to Fiona's consternation, incredibly handsome with a few stray locks of golden hair brushing across his forehead.

Stop noticing these things! He's like a brother to you. Nothing more.

Swallowing, she drew the crisp winter air into her lungs and stepped hesitantly forward. She glanced down at the tree. The trunk wasn't all that wide. "I'm sure I can manage it."

"Not at the risk of falling," he told her severely. And then, before she could find a response, he'd grabbed hold of her hand and pulled her closer.

A gasp flew from her lips when a deep sensation of warmth spiraled through her. "Chadwick!"

His palm found her back, urging her onward. "Yes?"

"There's no need for you to..." He released her hand and grabbed hold of her waist. "Oh!" And then she was being lifted, up and over to where Rachel stood watching with wide-eyed dismay.

"I grew tired of waiting," Chadwick explained, coming up beside them. "Shall we continue?"

Turning numbly, Fiona fell into step beside her sister while doing her best to settle her trembling nerves. Her heart was running away with her, and her skin felt all prickly, and...oh dear, she was probably succumbing to madness.

"This looks like an excellent spot to start,"

Rachel said when they arrived at a group of handsome pine trees all dusted with snow. She pulled a pruner from her pocket and set to work, providing two full branches in short succession.

Chadwick instantly bowed to help gather the pine in the baskets he'd brought, allowing Fiona to escape his notice by slipping between the trees to a more secluded spot. She needed to be alone with her contemplations and to add some distance to the man whose attention was rattling her brain. So she did what her sister had done and reached for her pruner, determined to distract herself from thoughts of Chadwick by focusing on her task. *Clip.* A fluffy bit of pine came away in her hand, the scent of it so intoxicating, she instinctively closed her eyes for a second and breathed it in.

Reluctantly, she set it aside and cut a few more, the pile at her feet increasing in size while bits of snow still clinging to the branches fell lazily to the ground.

Thwack!

Fiona jumped when a bit of cold wetness landed against the back of her neck. Spinning around while making sure she kept her balance in the slippery snow, she found Chadwick standing some distance away with a devilish gleam to his eyes and another snowball pressed neatly between his hands.

"I'll get you for that!"

Without thinking, Fiona started toward him while putting her pruner back in her pocket. He'd already turned away with a laugh, escaping between the thick branches of the trees while Fiona bent to gather up snow as she went. Spotting Rachel, who now held a knife to a larger branch,

Fiona surveyed the surrounding area for any sign of her quarry, only to find herself targeted once more from behind.

Determined to have her revenge, she turned around deftly and immediately noticed the sway of recently disturbed branches at her left. Hesitantly, she headed in that direction while glancing back over her shoulder every few paces. She would not allow herself to be surprised by him again. So she moved with careful adroitness, pushing between the pine trees until she spotted him further ahead. He appeared to be looking out from what he likely believed to be an excellent hiding place.

Smiling with glee, Fiona edged closer and knelt down, quietly forming additional snowballs until she had ten in total. And then, with a grin of devilish delight, she launched them at her opponent, sending them flying with remarkable accuracy, one after another.

"What the—" Turning around, Chadwick caught a missile square in the face. "Why you little—" *Thwack!* "You'd better run!"

Heedless of his threat, she continued throwing the balls at him until all had been used. That was when it occurred to her he was much closer now than he'd been before, and the mischief he wore on his features was likely to see a bit of snow shoved down the back of her gown.

Shuddering at the idea, she started to rise, but he was suddenly upon her, throwing her back against the snow while pinning her arms down and straddling her hips. "You're a monster. Do you know that?"

"You started it." Could she possibly sound more

childish?

He gave her a devilish look, immediately sucking all air from her lungs. "Fiona, Fiona, what will your punishment be? I know…" He moved her arms so he could hold her wrists in place with one hand. With the other, he started tickling her sides.

A squeal was her immediate response. He grinned with perverse delight and tickled her again until she was writhing from side to side, laughing and squealing and begging for mercy. Until he suddenly stopped. She opened her eyes and went instantly still at the sight of his dark expression. It was so foreign, she scarcely knew what to make of it. And then he suddenly pushed himself away and offered his hand to help her up.

"Is everything all right?" Rachel asked as she broke through between the trees. "I heard Fiona screaming and feared something tragic might have occurred."

"We were chasing each other about," Chadwick said. "Your sister can be quite vocal when she gets caught." His voice was tight, and Fiona became acutely aware that he was refusing to look at her. "I'll allow the two of you to finish your trimmings while I take a brief walk."

Fiona stared after him while Rachel remained at her side. For a moment there, she'd felt as though they were back to their usual pranks, but then it had ended, and she'd found herself lost and wrapped in a newfound alertness – the unfamiliar strength and power of a man's body pushing down on her own. And it was as though her blood had grown hot in her veins. Which made no sense at all since the man in question was Chadwick.

"I don't understand," she said, speaking to the vacant spot where Chadwick had stood seconds earlier.

A pause followed, and then Rachel quietly whispered, "Perhaps you ought to take some time to reevaluate the way in which you interact with him, Fiona. You're not the little girl you once were, and regardless of what you may think, he is hardly your brother."

CHAPTER FOUR

Ordinarily, Edward loved nothing better than participating in a lively game of charades. But that had been before he'd straddled Fiona in the forest and seen baffled awareness spring to life in the depths of her dark green eyes.

His arousal had struck him like a shovel to the back of the head. *Holy hell!* What the devil had he been thinking to allow such inappropriate contact between them? Obviously, he hadn't been using his head at all. That much was clear. He'd simply reacted on instinct until he'd been left with no choice but to add significant distance between them. Because the alternative…

He dared not even think of what that might have led to, not only because it would probably mean getting murdered by her six siblings but, more importantly, because he feared what it would do to his relationship with her. Revealing the way he truly felt would alter everything between them. And yet, the way she'd gazed up at him with slightly parted lips suggested she might finally be starting to view him in a different light.

She was young – only nineteen years to his thirty

– and yet, as much as he'd tried to consider other women over the course of the last few months, none of them had captured his attention the way she did. So he watched her now while she mimed her clues, either shaking her head or nodding in response to the eager guesses being made. Her hair was a wild collection of curls that he longed to unpin and watch fall down her back, her features so soft he'd always compared her to Da Vinci's depiction of the angel in Virgin of the Rocks. She was perfect in every way, the only woman with whom he envisioned forming an attachment. He loved her, damn it, so there could be no other. It had to be her, and only her.

"It's your turn," Emily said, forcing him out of his reverie. She stood before him, holding a box with one final piece of folded paper toward him.

He picked it up and glanced at it carefully, so the others would not be able to see. "You'll never guess this one," he said with exaggeration. Everyone loved the prankster in him, so that was what he'd deliver while keeping the sentimental romantic to himself. "I dare say it is quite impossible." Allowing a grin, he got to his feet and strode to the center of the room.

"We'll soon prove you wrong," Belgrave said with a laugh.

Laura clapped her hands. "Oh, indeed we shall."

Edward held up one finger.

"One word," Fiona called, leaning forward in her seat.

Rewarding her with a gentle smile, Edward nodded before spreading his hands and moving them in a square, cube-like, outline.

Emily jumped in her seat. "A box!"

Edward wiped his hand over his forehead to indicate she was on the right track. He then tugged on his ear.

"Rhymes with," Lady Oakland called out.

Pointing to the front of his throat, he glanced around the room and waited, a smile pulling at his lips while he watched their puzzled expressions. And then Fiona suddenly snapped her fingers together. "Adam's apple rhymes with a word for box. It's tabernacle!" She bounced in her seat, grinning with unabashed enthusiasm.

Edward gallantly bowed in her direction. "Well done, Imp." He'd deliberately used the endearment he'd given her when she was little, for it allowed him to remember she deserved a suitor closer to her own age. But when he raised his gaze and his eyes caught hers, he saw she had stilled. A look of confusion marred her features. It was almost as if she could not comprehend what he'd said.

"Well, that was fun," Emily said.

Laura stood. "I plan to put out some treats for the birds and squirrels down by the lake. Would anyone care to join me?"

"I think I could use some fresh air," Lamont said.

"I will go too," Rachel told her, after which Emily, Belgrave, and Montsmouth quickly joined the group.

"We'll take our afternoon naps then," Lady Oakland said, a wink directed at her husband.

Lady Duncaster chuckled. "Afternoon naps indeed." She exited the room, while Lady Oakland turned a deep shade of pink.

Edward smiled as the gathering dispersed. "What

about you?" he asked Fiona when he saw she remained behind. "Don't you wish to join them?"

A lovely rose-colored hue crept into her cheeks. "No. I believe our walk this morning has given me enough outdoor exercise for the day."

Edward's chest tightened. He felt his heart drum slightly faster as he watched her lick her lips in a nervous gesture that made him want to pull her into his arms and taste her. Instead, he remained where he was. "Well then…would you like to join me for a cup of tea?"

Her eyes brightened with sudden interest. "Let's order hot chocolate instead." She went to the bell pull and called for a maid. "Shall we sit by the fire?"

"Of course." He followed her over while trying to figure out how best to escape the stilted atmosphere that seemed to have settled between them. If only things could go back to the way they'd once been. If only he hadn't knocked her onto her back and climbed over her. "About this morning," he said while she lowered herself to the loveseat facing the fireplace.

Tilting her head, she looked up at him with eyes that threatened to be his undoing. No woman should be permitted to look at a man with such innocent obliviousness. "What about it?"

Realizing this would likely be one of those exhaustingly awkward conversations, Edward sighed heavily and sank down beside her. He should probably have claimed the adjacent armchair, but his craving for closeness with her would not be denied. Not when the door stood respectably open, and there was no risk of a scandal. Just as long as he kept his hands to himself. He folded them in his lap.

A maid entered the room. "How may I be of service?" she asked.

Fiona placed their order, and Edward waited until the maid had departed before saying, "I crossed the line. It won't happen again."

She drew a sharp breath, paused for a second, and then expelled it. "We were only playing. I see no harm in it."

Perhaps not for her. He gritted his teeth. "Fiona, I am a grown man, and you are no longer a child, but a debutante in her first Season. For me to fall on you like I did and tickle you silly was horribly wrong. I apologize for it, truly I do."

Biting her lip, she worried the plump piece of flesh while Edward reached for the armrest, his fingers clutching the wood like a vice. "Is our fun at an end then?"

"No." How could she possibly think that? "I shall always be your partner in mischief."

The maid reappeared carrying a tray filled with cups, a large pot of hot chocolate, and a plate with some slices of cake. She set it down on the table before them, bobbed a curtsy, and took her leave. Fiona reached for the pot and started to pour. "I sense things are changing between us," she whispered, "and I'm not so sure I like it."

"Consider it the price of growing up, Fiona. You cannot continue to play the child, and I cannot continue to indulge you."

"Is that what you've been doing for all of these years?" She handed him his cup, her eyes wide with interest.

"No," he confessed. Trying to drink, he almost

scalded himself in the process, so he set the cup aside and turned enough to face her. "I have always enjoyed your company tremendously. In fact…the difference in age never felt like an issue."

Until now.

She smiled at him over the rim of her own cup. Her lips parted slightly so she could blow on her drink before taking a sip.

Edward held his breath while he followed the movement, his blood heating in his veins as he watched her swallow. *Christ!* He would never be able to drink hot chocolate again without finding it highly erotic.

"I have always considered you to be my dearest friend," she said, lowering the cup. "When I told you I wished to find my great aunt's jewelry box during my stay here this past summer, my entire family tried to dissuade me. But you didn't."

"I know how important finding it is to you."

She nodded and placed her cup on the table. "Perhaps…" Shaking her head, she turned in her seat, enough for her knee to brush his.

An overwhelming dart of pleasure rushed up his thigh, tightening his limbs and rendering him speechless.

"What if I were to tell you that I intend to continue my hunt while I'm here?" she asked.

Blinking, Edward tried to focus his lust-infused brain on what she'd just told him. "I'd say you do not lack determination."

She grinned, bright and lovely. "You're right. When I set my mind to something, nothing can make me give up."

If only she'd set her mind to him then, he mused,

cad that he was. He banked the baser urges she stirred in him. "Perhaps I can help."

"Oh, Edward!" Reaching for his hands, she grasped them between her own while pure appreciation gleamed in her eyes. "I would love for us to go on this adventure together."

Edward's throat went dry. In spite of their closeness, he'd always been Chadwick to all of the Heartlys. Not Edward. Never Edward. Until now. This was the first time Fiona had used his given name. He wondered if she was even aware of the fact. Probably not.

Nodding numbly, he murmured, "So would I."

He forced his most rapscallion smile in order to distract himself from the warmth of her fingers still holding his. There were no gloves between them, nothing but skin against skin, so enticing he was sorely tempted to pull her onto his lap and give her a lesson or two in the art of kissing.

Instead, he withdrew his hands from hers – sweet torture that it was – and offered her a slice of cake. She took it happily, eating it with a certain degree of enthusiasm that instantly made him smile.

"Can we begin our hunt right away?" she asked a few minutes later. "Given our limited time here, I don't want to lose a second."

"Of course." He rose to his feet, relieved to add some distance between them. "Where would you like to start?"

"Well, my greataunt's earring was found in one of the tunnels leading toward the sea. And then there's the underground Roman villa Richard and Mary found."

"They said it served as headquarters for the Cardinals – some sort of resistance movement your greataunt, grandfather, and Lord Duncaster were all a part of?"

"That's right. A letter found by Mary and notes kept by my grandfather suggest their codenames were the North Wind, the South Wind, and the East Wind. We still don't know who the West Wind might have been, but perhaps we can find some information about that as we search."

"If we're lucky." He didn't want to get her hopes up in case they failed to find anything at all.

She gave him a look of distinct disappointment. "Please don't give up before we've begun."

"I will do my best to help you in your quest, Fiona, you needn't worry about that."

"Good, because there's also the journal Chloe and Stonegate found in the attic – the one outlining the members and deeds of the evil Electors – the men against whom the Cardinals fought."

"I doubt we need to concern ourselves with them since Stonegate ensured they were all arrested."

"Agreed," Fiona said, "but it does go to show that clues might be found in any part of the manor. There's no indication of where the treasure is hidden, but if we piece together what we already know, an image does begin to emerge."

Fascinated by her attempts at deduction, Edward considered her closely. "How so?"

She stood and started to pace. "We know from my grandmother's journal that my grandfather came here one night in order to retrieve a box. I propose she was referring to her sister's jewelry box, which was sent from France when the Duchess of Marveille feared for her life. She did not wish for it to fall into the wrong hands. But when Grandpapa arrived here, something happened – something that prompted him to set out to sea with Lord Duncaster instead of returning home to his wife. Their ship was lost, both men drowned, but I doubt they would have taken the box out to sea with them when it was meant to be delivered to Grandmamma. Which means it must still be here since she never received it."

"I suppose that sounds reasonable."

She smiled and met his gaze. "What if the earring in the corridor below fell from the box after arrival? Perhaps Lord Duncaster tripped while carrying it, and a piece was lost. After that, he would have taken the stairs to the interior courtyard. No doubt, his intention would have been to hide the box in the underground villa, but time was of the essence – he would have wanted to make my grandfather aware of its arrival. So he stopped by his study first in order to pen a letter, temporarily hiding it somewhere there."

"Once the letter was dispatched, how long do you suppose it might have taken your grandfather to arrive here?"

"His estate wasn't far, perhaps an hour at a fast gallop."

"So that would have given Lord Duncaster at least two hours in which to move the box elsewhere, possibly to the villa as you suggest."

"Except it did not end up there. I gave the place a thorough look after Richard showed it to me."

Edward considered this bit of information with interest. "And we also know something must have happened immediately after your grandfather's arrival here to prompt both him and Lord Duncaster to flee."

Fiona nodded. "I believe the Electors discovered who the Cardinals were, and they came to kill them."

"The fourth one though, the West Wind. Do you think there's a chance he might still be alive?"

"I honestly can't say. As for the box, I suspect it is somewhere here on the ground level, either between Lord Duncaster's study and the interior courtyard, or closer to the front entrance."

"The parts of the manor he would have crossed before setting back out to sea."

"Precisely." She paused, her gaze locked with his, and it was almost as if she was waiting for him to react in some way, to close the distance between them and…what? She couldn't possibly want the same as he, a bold and passionate embrace wrought with hunger and desire.

So he strode toward the door instead and gestured with his hand. "It seems our adventure awaits, my lady." Smiling cheekily, he dipped his head and quietly added, "After you."

CHAPTER FIVE

BALANCING ON THE THIRD RUNG of a spindly library ladder, Rachel reached for the thick leather-bound volume she'd come to find: *Elements of Chemistry*, translated from French by Robert Kerr. Carefully, she pulled it off the shelf, aware that the weight of it would soon threaten to put her off balance. So she braced her feet against the side rails and leaned into the ladder. The book came free, almost slipping from between her fingers as she tried to secure a stronger hold on it.

"What do you have there?"

Startled by the presence of another person standing immediately behind her, Rachel gasped and dropped the book, helplessly watching its rapid descent until a hand suddenly swooped out and caught it. Rachel turned to find Belgrave studying its title.

"My lord." Slowly, she stepped down off the ladder only to realize the viscount now had her at a disadvantage for his height was far superior to her own. She gestured toward the book. "If I may?"

Lifting his gaze, he allowed a couple of seconds to elapse while studying her closely – so closely she couldn't help but shift her feet. Still, she refused to look away, unwilling to cower beneath his direct perusal.

"Do you ever indulge in fiction, my lady?" He allowed her to retrieve her prize while tilting his head as though trying to comprehend her.

Instinctively, she tightened her jaw and raised her chin so she could look at him more fully. "No."

"Hmm…" His eyes remained locked with hers. "Why am I not surprised?"

"I cannot possibly imagine."

A dimple appeared at the edge of his mouth, and then he suddenly smiled, the brightness of it infusing his eyes with a deep blue tone reminiscent of midnight. His hair was swept to one side with a few rebellious strands brushing his brow in a manner that tempted her to reach out and put them to rights. Controlling the urge, she became increasingly aware of her own drab appearance. She was like a boring little field mouse when compared to his dashing good looks. The idea gave her pause, and she took a step back, unnerved by the notion that she'd never wasted a second on such superficiality before.

"If you'll excuse me."

She meant to move past him, but he stuck out his arm, trapping her between it and the ladder. Slowly, he lowered it with the unspoken request that she stay where she was. "Please." Turning slightly, he gestured toward a quiet corner filled with comfortable-looking chairs. "Won't you join me for a bit?"

"I…" No man had ever invited her to sit with him before, and it put her quite out of her depth.

Her nerves, which were generally made of steel, felt fragile, unpleasantly quivering and quaking. She clutched the book in front of her chest. "I'm not—"

"Perhaps you can tell me more about your interests?" He nodded toward the book. "Your scientific studies?"

"My lord, you cannot possibly mean to find my thoughts enticing enough to warrant such interest on your part." There had to be an angle – an ulterior motive.

He studied her gravely and then leaned in, close enough for her to catch the scent of bergamot and leather. It did something to her senses, something heady she could not quite understand. One thing was certain: her heart beat faster against the inexplicable tightening of her stays, and she was suddenly quite incapable of speech.

"You do me a great injustice." He spoke in a rich timbre that curled its way through her. "To presume I will not understand the ideas you might put forth is—"

"My lord?" She blinked in quick succession. "You think I believe myself intellectually superior to you? That this is the cause for my reluctance?" It seemed incredulous that a man of his superb character would doubt himself in her company.

"Is that not what you were implying?"

She gaped at him. "No! I merely meant to suggest you would regret engaging me in conversation, not because you lack the mental faculty to comprehend me, but because I am not…" She lost her momentum and sighed.

"You are not?" he prompted, raising both eyebrows in question.

"My lord, you must agree I am not a terribly fascinating person."

A frown appeared on his brow. "Who told you that?"

She couldn't help but laugh. "I am perfectly aware of my lacking elegance, refinement, and beauty. I am not as accomplished as my sisters, nor as lively or prone to good cheer. Life is like an equation to me, one I am constantly trying to puzzle through."

"And this keeps you serious? It demands a degree of focus that will not allow for humor?"

"Exactly." She was so glad he understood.

"And yet I have seen you smile and laugh at least once during the course of this conversation, so I daresay you might be less stern than you think yourself to be." He allowed his eyes to drift over her so slowly, strange little fluttering sensations sprang to life in her belly. Returning his gaze to hers, he said, "As for the part about elegance, refinement, and beauty, I can assure you you're quite mistaken."

"My lord, I—"

"Please, let's not quarrel any further over trivialities. As it is, we have already stood here for a good ten minutes according to the clock on that table. Why not rest our feet for a while?" He gestured once more toward the seating arrangement.

Rachel hesitated. If only she could manage to escape without being rude. Because the way he made her feel… Good lord, it was more unnerving than the idea of one day presenting an invention to the Royal Society in the hope of being admitted. Still, the thought of talking to someone who seemed willing to listen was tempting.

"Very well," she agreed.

They crossed the floor, and he waited until she was comfortably seated before asking, "Would you care for some refreshment? I can call for a maid and ask for some tea or lemonade to be brought up."

Pressing her lips together, Rachel wondered how much more of herself she might reveal before he went running in the opposite direction. She decided to test his resolve in keeping her company and quietly said, "A brandy would be my preference, if you're willing to indulge me."

His lips quirked with amusement, and he turned toward a nearby table with a rich selection of bottles. "So full of surprises," he murmured, filling two glasses. "Tell me, do you also fence?"

Pleased with his response, she allowed a smile of her own, though it was directed at his back. "No," she admitted, "I prefer archery and shooting. Indeed, I take great pride in calculating the trajectory of each shot I fire."

"Good God." He turned to her with a laugh, spilling a bit of the drink in the process. "To think you haven't been snatched up yet by a gentleman seeking adventure."

She snorted, accepting the glass he handed to her. "I am hardly the sort of lady to offer such a thing to any man."

"Hmph." Brushing his coattails out from behind him, he lowered himself to the chair closest to hers. "You sell yourself short, Lady Rachel, for indeed, I can think of no greater adventure than inventing the future while engaging in bloodthirsty sport." He smiled broadly over the rim of his glass, held her gaze for a moment, and then took a hasty sip.

She drank as well, if for no other reason than to settle the butterflies in her stomach.

"Do you have other experiments in mind beside the electric arc?" Belgrave asked. He leaned back in his chair and nodded toward her book.

Crossing his legs, he held his glass between his hands while studying her with an intense degree of focus she'd never before been subjected to. It filled her with an unusual sense of importance – made her feel as though she mattered when she was more accustomed to fading away in the background.

"Of course." Now that she'd been invited to speak, she hardly knew where to begin. "I've successfully followed Priestley's guidelines on how to isolate oxygen, and I've conducted numerous experiments on the conservation of mass as proposed by Antoine Lavoisier, the author of that book." She indicated the volume with a wave of her hand before taking another sip of her drink. The brandy immediately soothed her insides.

"What does it entail?"

"It's quite simple, really." She smoothed her skirts in an effort to ease her pulse with a menial task. "The law states that in a closed system, the reactants will weigh the same as the product."

"In other words, if you were to heat a block of ice in a sealed container until it was fully melted, the weight of the container and its contents would remain unchanged?"

"That's right. But if the system is open, mass is lost. What I mean to discover is why, since I refuse to believe it simply disappears. No. I suspect it transforms into some sort of gas."

"Into oxygen perhaps?"

"I don't think so, but the only way to find out is to somehow isolate it. The most fascinating part of my hypothesis is that its mass must equal the amount lost in the final product."

He dipped his head. "What fascinates me, aside from your brilliant brain, is how you have managed to conduct your experiments without your parents realizing what you were up to."

"I acquired a small stove for my bedchamber," Rachel confessed. "It remains covered when not in use, and since I only work at night…To be honest, the fault is my own. I don't make a habit of sharing my fondness for science with others."

"And yet, you chose to do so with me."

She found it impossible to look at him all of a sudden, for he'd lowered his voice to a sensual tone that tempted her with something she'd never wanted before – something she'd never dared hope might be hers.

"Your attentiveness was difficult to ignore."

A bit of silence slid into place, and she suddenly felt an urgent need to flee from this man before she played the fool and wished for something that could never possibly be. Because as interesting as he might find her intellectually, she knew she wasn't the sort of woman to inspire deep emotion in anyone. After all, she did own a mirror, so she was fairly certain that whatever compliment he'd paid her earlier about her beauty had been done so out of kindness rather than honesty. So she stood and snatched up the book while he looked at her in confusion.

"If you'll please excuse me," she said, "I fear I've kept you long enough." She turned and walked away quickly, acknowledging that the lady who won Lord Belgrave's affection would be a lucky woman indeed.

CHAPTER SIX

DRESSED FOR SUPPER, ARTHUR RODERICK Compton, Viscount Belgrave, descended the grand staircase that curled around the central hall and headed toward the green parlor where the rest of the party gathered.

"I wish we were able to use the themed salons while we're here," Lady Laura was saying as he made his entrance. She stood with Lady Duncaster, closest to the door, while the Oaklands, Lady Emily and Lady Fiona, along with Chadwick, Lamont, and Montsmouth gathered in clusters behind them, filling the space with their chatter.

"So do I, my dear," Lady Duncaster told her. She glanced in Arthur's direction, acknowledging his arrival with a smile. "But heating all of this space for so few guests would be rather impractical. Just think of all the wood we'd require!"

"And to be fair," Arthur said, coming to a halt before them, "this room with its vibrant carpets decorating the floors and sofas dressed in rich burgundy velvet, the glow of candlelight warming the walls and the faint crackle of wood burning in the fireplace lends a degree of intimacy I very much do favor."

"What a remarkable compliment," Lady Duncaster said. A twinkle lit her eyes. "And in case we do experience a particularly chilly evening and the fire isn't enough, I have ensured there are enough blankets in here for everyone to cozy up with."

"But the salons," Lady Laura insisted. "They are so unique and…"

Whatever she said next was lost on Arthur as his attention was drawn to a movement off to one side. Instinctively, he shifted his gaze to see Lady Rachel step into the room. Her gown was plain as usual – a fawn muslin creation that seemed too bland for her complexion. But she'd done something different with her hair, he noted. There were curls in it tonight, soft and alluring. Two framed the sides of her face in a way that accentuated her beauty. And she *was* beautiful, even though she'd been doing her best to hide it.

Not now though. Something had changed. Whatever it was, it had made her slightly more daring and perhaps even eager to draw favorable attention. Arthur could only hope he might have been the cause of her transformation. It was the damnedest thing really, because he'd scarcely noticed her during the summer, perhaps because his attentions had been elsewhere. But now, with so few people present, he'd had the opportunity to become better acquainted with Lady Rachel and was stunned to discover how attractive he found her. She was so sharp and bold, unlike any other lady he'd ever encountered, and he very much wanted to cultivate whatever connection that flourished between them.

"If you'll excuse me," he murmured, politely taking his leave of his two companions before moving toward the woman who'd caught his interest.

"My lady." He kept his voice deliberately low as he came to a halt before her. She stared at him with big round eyes, like a rabbit caught in a snare. Touched by her wariness, he offered his arm. A pause followed, and he could practically hear her mind warring with uncertainty. Eventually, to his relief, she accepted his escort, and he slowly guided her further into the room. Dipping his head ever so slightly, he whispered for her ears alone, "I feel compelled to compliment you on your beauty this evening. Indeed, I believe you have managed to outshine your sisters."

Her breath hitched and she tugged on her arm, but he refused to yield to her fears and kept her snug against him instead. Eventually, he felt the tension within her subside, and she surrendered to his desire for continued closeness. "There is no need for you to fill my head with false compliments, my lord. Telling me you're aware of my increased effort to style my hair in a more flattering manner would have sufficed."

He couldn't help but smile in response to her stubbornness – her refusal to see herself as the gem she truly was. The compulsion to show her precisely how lovely he considered her assailed him in a flash. His stomach tightened with the sudden awareness of it, of her, and… Dear God, he was not a scoundrel or a libertine. He was a gentleman – good, honorable, kind. And yet, there was something about Lady Rachel's prim attire contrasted with her pretty coiffure that made him dream about tearing her clothes off with his teeth, of running his fingers through her hair until she looked wild and wanton, her eyes aglow with desire while…

"My lord?" She was staring up at him with a quizzical expression.

"Hmm?"

She frowned. "Should we not join the others?"

Confused by her question, he glanced around, surprised to discover they were alone. What the devil? "Where did everyone go?"

"To the dining room, I suspect. Supper was called a minute ago. Did you not hear?"

"No." He'd been in a daze. One he'd rather not tell her about at present. "My apologies, Lady Rachel. Allow me to lead you on through."

Joining the rest of the guests, they claimed the last remaining chairs. He helped her sit before lowering himself into the seat beside her. Wine was poured, and a lively discussion soon began at the head of the table as Lady Duncaster and Lord Oakland spoke of the late duke and Lord Oakland's parents. They had clearly been close friends, and with Lady Duncaster one of the last surviving members of that generation, Arthur could tell she provided the earl with a sentimental link to a time he was more than eager to revisit. It made Arthur think of his own parents – of how dearly he still missed his father after all of these years and how difficult it had to be for his mother to go on without him.

Intent on disrupting the maudlin mood enveloping him, he addressed Lady Rachel while plates filled with some sort of fish topped with lemon and dill were set before them. Arthur stared at it before quietly saying, "I wonder if I can get away with eating only the lemon."

"What?" Lady Rachel sounded confused.

Lowering his voice, he whispered, "I've never been overly fond of scaly creatures."

The barest hint of a smile touched her lips. "You would rather eat an animal that's soft and gentle with innocent eyes and a trusting nature?" She stuck a piece of fish in her mouth without the barest hint of liking it or not.

"I enjoy the flavor, though I'd rather not think of where the meat came from. Attending a dinner where the whole pig is laid out on the table is not to my taste either, but…" He stared down at his plate for a second before looking at her again. "When I was a lad, my parents and I travelled to visit my uncle. We stopped at a tavern along the way for a meal, and since it was near a seaside village, fish was ordered. I got a bone stuck in my throat – took forever to get the thing out."

"So you swore never to eat fish again."

"I did." Recalling the prickly feel of the bone still made him shudder.

"Well," she remarked, "I suppose that's logical. Cause and effect, and so forth."

"Have you always been so frank in your statements?"

She shrugged, and another piece of fish went into her mouth. "I think so, though my memory only stretches back to the age of three, so I honestly can't be sure."

That made him laugh. She didn't even bat an eyelash, however, which prompted him to wonder if she was aware of her dry sense of humor.

He chose not to question it, determined, rather, to learn more about her. "Tell me, for I am curious." He started cutting his food. Not because he would eat any of it, but because simply sitting there with his hands in his lap seemed wrong. "How will you create this electrical lamp you plan on inventing?"

A frown appeared upon her brow, and for a long moment, she remained completely silent. Then, as if in a trance, she turned her head to face him. "What is your ulterior motive, my lord?"

He almost choked on the bit of wine he'd been sipping. "Ulterior motive?"

"You seek me out, make conversation, flatter me with compliments that common sense prevents me from believing though my vanity would certainly like to." She stared at him as though she was trying to pick him apart. "Nobody has ever wanted to know my scientific mind, not even my own family."

"Lady Rachel—"

"So. What is it you're truly after?"

Christ! If the woman was so intent on being suspicious, he'd have to find a different way to connect with her. "You," he told her simply. He allowed her to gape at him for a full ten seconds before saying, "If you do not wish to discuss your work, then by all means, let us talk about the weather or agriculture. Horses and fashion are equally riveting, of course. I'll let you choose. And if you ever decide you're willing to trust me a little, I'll listen to your theories and ideas with enthusiasm. Until then, please know I find you delightfully unique, and I intend to pursue you with every intention of seeking marriage."

What the hell was that *he just said?*

Something about marriage, if his memory served and her shocked expression was anything to go by. Oh yes, he was in deep now, deeper than he'd ever been before, and yet he didn't regret a single word he'd uttered, however spontaneous he'd been. Because the fact was, he needed a wife – he was more than ready for a wife – and Lady Rachel… Her genius promised him a lifetime of fascination filled with thought-provoking conversation. What sensible man would walk away from that?

"Why?" She appeared adorably flummoxed, her wide eyes displaying every nuance of brown that had ever existed.

"Because I like you," he admitted, "and because I would be a fool to hesitate and allow another man to claim you."

Her lips suddenly trembled, and then she laughed, bright and beautiful in the confines of the room, a sound so unusual everyone else fell silent while they paused to listen. She glanced about at the puzzled expressions on everyone's faces. But her smile didn't falter. It remained on her lips as she shook her head with an uncharacteristic girlishness that made Arthur's heart swell.

"Are you all right?" Lady Oakland inquired of her daughter.

Lady Rachel nodded. "Oh yes, Mama. Quite." To Arthur, she discreetly whispered, "Though I do believe you must be cracked in the head."

He snorted in protest while doing his best not to laugh as well.

"I can't recall ever seeing you laugh with such abandon before," Lady Emily said. She turned a curious gaze on Arthur. "If this is your doing, my lord, then I am pleased indeed."

"As am I," Lady Fiona put in.

"Hear, hear," Lord Oakland added, raising his glass in salute.

Arthur raised his as well and waited for the rest of the guests to follow suit. "To spending Christmas with friends," he said. His toast was echoed and everyone drank. The fish was removed and replaced with venison, accompanied by roasted potatoes, vegetables, and gravy.

"We shall need a yule log soon," Lady Duncaster remarked, after making plans to continue with the Christmas decorations the following day. Enough had been made to fill the parlor, the garlands providing a pretty border of green along the edges of the ceiling, but more had yet to be crafted for the dining room.

"Perhaps Lady Rachel and I can manage the task tomorrow." Ignoring Lady Rachel's whispered, "No," he looked directly at Lord Oakland. "With your permission, of course."

"I have no objection," the earl said. "Not as long as you take a chaperone with you."

Arthur nodded. "Naturally."

"Have I no say in the matter?" Lady Rachel asked in a quiet voice intended only for Arthur. She sounded as though his company was the last thing on earth she might consider seeking.

And yet, he sensed she was not as immune to him as she was letting on. Discreetly, he moved his leg – enough to allow for their knees to touch. He felt her flinch, but she remained where she was, refusing to move away. A distinct flush began to rise up her neck, and he could tell her breathing had slowed. So he leaned slightly sideways, intent on disrupting her even further by saying, "Why deny yourself what you secretly crave?"

"I…I…"

"Surrender, my lady, and I can assure you that you will be pleased you did so."

She made a strangled sort of sound when he leaned back, adding distance. Purposefully, he returned his attention to his meal, aware he'd lit a dangerous fuse and that there was no telling when an explosion might follow.

CHAPTER SEVEN

SETTING HER QUILL ASIDE, LAURA sprinkled some red blotting sand across the page she'd just finished writing. She snuffed out the candle at the corner of her escritoire, for there was no longer a need for it, now that the sun had risen. Stretching, she considered returning to bed for a morning nap, but doing so would probably result in missing breakfast, and if she were honest, she was actually more hungry than tired.

So she rang for a maid to help her dress and then headed toward the stairs, her mind so preoccupied with the next chapter of the book she was working on, she failed to notice the man who approached from the other end of the hallway until he was suddenly directly before her.

"Lady Laura," the Duke of Lamont spoke with a grave expression that made her feel like a naughty child about to be chastised. "I wasn't aware you're an early riser as well."

"Perhaps because I tend to return to my bed at this time for another couple of hours." She hoped she wasn't being too blunt. Intent on softening her tone, she said, "Today is an exception, mostly because I am eager to indulge in breakfast. I've missed it for the last few days."

The edge of his mouth quirked, and she felt compelled to follow the movement. It brought her attention straight to his mouth, and she realized as she studied it closely that it was far more sensual than she ever would have imagined, given his otherwise angular features and somber demeanor. His eyes were warm, though they held a haunted element to them. It made her wonder about the scar he wore on his soul. It was common knowledge he'd suffered after the war. What man wouldn't have after losing his father and brother in an unexpected accident?

"I was actually going to go for an early ride myself, but perhaps I'll accompany you instead. If you will allow it?"

"Certainly, Your Grace." She'd received attention from gentlemen before but not from someone as powerful as Lamont. The idea of him potentially taking a fancy to her was, of course, ridiculous. Obviously, her romantic nature was overruling her logical mind. A man of his distinction would want a wife refined enough to fill the position of duchess, not someone who couldn't even manage to keep the ink stains from her fingers.

He offered his arm and she accepted. "Have you been working on one of your novels?" he asked, acknowledging the black blotches that tainted her skin. Walking side by side, they started down the stairs.

Oh, if only she'd taken better care to clean it off before venturing out of her room. "You know I am an author?" It was a little surprising since she'd only recently been published and in a genre she doubted he'd have any interest in.

"Yes." He kept silent while they descended two more steps, then quietly admitted, "I have recently read *The Lady Risks It All* and—"

She drew to a halt. "You have?" Keeping her surprise from her voice was impossible.

He looked down at her with a seriousness that made her wonder if he would ever smile in her presence. And she suddenly wished she had it in her to make him do so, even as his eyes held hers with an intensity that made her feel slightly lightheaded. "I enjoyed it. Your wit in the dialogues, the lavish descriptions, and the struggles both protagonists have to overcome in order to find happiness were riveting."

"Riveting?" She could scarcely fathom how well the compliment pleased her.

"Well, yes. Does that surprise you?"

"Actually," she would be honest with him, "it does rather. I never would have imagined a man might wish to read what I've written."

"Then you do not give yourself enough credit." He tugged her arm gently, and they resumed walking. "I was wondering," he said, once they were half way down, "if you might like to join my wards and me later. I have promised to spend some time with them today."

The proposal caught her completely off guard, for she'd barely recovered from the knowledge that he had actually read her book. Oh, to think he'd caught such a private insight of her mind – her secret passions, her hopes, and her dreams – was unnerving to say the least. "I—"

"Please say yes." They reached the bottom of the stairs and began making their way toward the dining room at a gradual pace.

She smiled up at him. A flicker of resolve in the confines of his eyes alerted her to an underlying urgency well hidden beneath his cool façade. "Very well," she agreed, and she immediately felt him relax. "But I must warn you, I have no experience with children."

"You have six siblings."

"Who are all fully grown."

"Touché." He allowed the faintest hint of a smile. It tugged at the edge of his lips. "Still, you needn't worry. Beatrice and Gemma are easy to get along with. I don't foresee any issues."

"Perhaps not," she said. They reached the dining room and stepped inside. "But you might not like the favor I wish to ask of you in return."

Releasing her arm, he moved in order to face her more fully, blocking her from those who were already present at the table: her parents and Rachel. "Name it," he told her. His hands were clasped behind his back, his head dipped slightly toward her as he spoke in a velvety voice that made her insides turn to goo.

Bracing herself for his refusal, she met his gaze squarely and said, "Come ice-skating with me later today." His hesitation, or horror, was instantly apparent in the tightly drawn lines of his face. He opened his mouth, no doubt intent on protesting, so she hastily added, "Please." She couldn't fathom why his agreement in this was so important, but the activity was one she'd always enjoyed and perhaps…perhaps if he could find joy in it too, he'd forget the troubles weighing heavily upon his shoulders.

It took a few seconds, but he eventually nodded. "Very well. I will do it." And then, in a much quieter voice that almost sounded seductive, he said, "But only because you are the one who is asking."

Her heart practically leapt into her throat while her stomach felt as though it was turning into syrup. *Silly girl*. He was merely being kind and attentive – a proper duke who'd simply addled her brain with his charm. To read more into it was beyond foolish. Especially since he scarcely considered her again during breakfast, his interest entirely captured by her father. *He* was able to engage Lamont in the sort of conversation she would never be able to enjoy with anyone, since she'd never had a firm understanding of politics. Not that ladies were supposed to discuss such things, but she'd always believed it might be useful to at least comprehend the basics in order to better connect with the man she eventually married. Unfortunately, she'd long since realized that to suppose such a thing would be useless. She simply didn't have the mind for it.

Distracting herself with the food, Laura devoured several pieces of bacon, two eggs, and a slice of toast. She was finishing off with a sip of tea when Lamont met her gaze. "Shall we?"

"The duke has asked me to join him and his charges today," Laura explained to her parents, who were both looking extremely curious. Rachel paid her no mind, her attention fixed on Lord Belgrave, who'd recently arrived.

"Then by all means," her mother said with a bright smile, "you mustn't let us keep you."

Acknowledging the comment with a nod, Laura rose and followed Lamont from the room. "I was thinking," she said as soon as they were alone once more, "that Beatrice and Gemma might enjoy making Christmas decorations. There are still a few more garlands left to tie with ribbons, and we can also make some paper flowers."

"I love how creative you are."

His eyes twinkled ever so slightly as he said it, and once again she found herself thinking of him in a different light – in a please-kiss-me-and-I'll-be-yours-forever kind of light. She had to stop these fanciful notions from creeping into her head. It couldn't possibly be healthy.

"This is Lady Laura," Lamont announced when they entered a sparse room Lady Duncaster had allocated as nursery. There were two sofas, a table, and a carpet on which various games had been strewn about. One of the two girls present was having a marvelous time with a rocking horse. The other lay on her belly, feet kicking in the air, while she drew a picture. Both jumped to attention at the sound of Lamont's voice.

Curtsies followed, and then, "Pleased to make your acquaintance," was spoken in unison.

Laura cast a hesitant glance in the duke's direction, just in time to see the pleased expression on his face. She gave her attention back to the girls. "It's a pleasure to make yours." She stepped further into the room. "I am hoping to join you today, if you'll let me." She heard Lamont's sharp intake of breath as he no doubt prepared to argue her intention to let the girls decide. Her hand reached out and grabbed hold of his arm, and the words he might have spoken immediately died on his lips.

"That depends," Beatrice said. She looked Laura critically up and down.

"On what?" Laura asked.

"On whether or not you're any fun."

Doing her best to keep a straight face in the light of such an important criteria being pronounced, Laura lowered herself to a squat so she was at eye level with the twins. "I thought we might make Christmas decorations while drinking hot chocolate and eating petit fours."

"What are petit fours?" Gemma asked.

"Little pastries filled with decadent cream and covered in an icing so rich it melts on your tongue."

The twins' eyes gleamed while smiles spread across their eager faces. "That sounds like a brilliant plan," Beatrice exclaimed, and Gemma nodded.

"I'm glad you approve," Laura told them. "I'll place the order and send word to a footman about the supplies we'll be requiring." She rose, her gaze colliding with Lamont's as she did so, and for a second her feet failed to move in the direction she needed to go. He was looking at her with a mixture of deep respect, gratitude, and... Surely not. For a man as solemn as he to regard a woman like her with such undeniable interest could not be possible. Could it? Her doubts increased as he schooled his features and went to study the picture Gemma had drawn.

Flustered and feeling terribly flushed, Laura rang for the maid, who arrived soon after. The footman she'd called returned a short while later carrying baskets filled with all kinds of supplies, and pine bundled under one arm. For the next hour, Laura immersed herself in the task of teaching Beatrice and Gemma how to make paper flowers. "They look marvelous," she told them sincerely when they both managed to produce their first set on their own.

"Perhaps you can help me with this garland now?" Lamont asked. He'd been told to tie branches of pine together with red silk ribbons. "These bows are proving a nuisance."

"Men are terrible at tying bows," Gemma said. She deftly tied one of her own, attaching one flower to another.

"Your confidence in my abilities is most endearing," Lamont told her dryly. The edge of humor to his tone was unmistakable, and when Laura looked at him, she saw he was finally smiling while concentrating on his work.

She sat beside him on the sofa. "Allow me to assist."

"If you'll hold this together here." He showed her where with his own hands. "It will make tying it easier."

She moved to do what he asked and then paused, aware she wouldn't be able to grab the loose sprigs without touching him in the process. Swallowing, she edged slightly closer and did as he bade. An immediate spark of pleasure ignited her flesh when her skin brushed against his. His sharp inhale suggested he felt it too. His hands retreated slowly, drawing out the moment of contact until her chest tightened and heat erupted in her veins.

Unable to look at him for fear of what she might see, she kept her gaze firmly upon the garland they were making. But when he began to wrap the ribbon around it, his fingers invariably touched hers. The feelings they stirred – the unexpected need for greater contact – confounded her. Yes, she wrote of great romance and enduring love, but she had never imagined she would ever feel like this.

"Thank you," he murmured while he tied the last bow.

Licking her lips, Laura tried to quell her frantic nerves. She felt as though she'd been cast into a turbulent storm and was unable to find a foothold. "It was my pleasure," she told him demurely. What else could she say? To comprehend the effect he'd had on her… She shifted, adding more distance between them, and then hazarded a look at his face. He was watching her closely – so closely it burned.

"Would it disturb you if…" He paused, broke eye contact for a second before looking at her again. "If I told you I had no intention of accepting Lady Duncaster's invitation until I discovered you would be here."

"But spending Christmas with her has become something of a tradition for you in recent years. Has it not?"

"Yes, but I was actually planning to celebrate at my own estate this year. I thought it might be fun for Beatrice and Gemma to try planning the festivities. When I heard you would be visiting Thorncliff, however, I couldn't stay away."

The admission was overwhelming. "I don't know what to say." The words barely whispered past her lips.

He winced. "No. I don't suppose you would."

"Your Grace, I cannot think what reason you might have had to—"

"Can't you?" He'd grabbed her hand with startling swiftness, his eyes wilder than she'd ever thought possible as he cast a quick glance at the twins, ensuring they were preoccupied with their work, before leaning toward her. "You have my highest regard, my lady, more so after—"

"Uncle?" Beatrice's voice stopped him from proceeding. Slowly, he released Laura's hand and stood, his focus now on his little charges, who were holding up their paper flowers. "What do you think? Aren't they pretty?"

"Indeed they are," he assured them while Laura watched with an ache in her heart. "But not nearly as pretty as you."

He might not show pleasure in a physical way, but the duke's ability to love was very much apparent in his treatment of his nieces. Each received a kiss on the cheek, and his attention never wavered from them while they showed him how each flower was made. And in that moment, Laura felt herself overcome by emotion. This man didn't love her. How could he, after a few brief encounters? But the possibility for it was there, waiting to be explored.

CHAPTER EIGHT

AFTER PARTING WAYS WITH LADY Laura immediately after luncheon with the promise of reconvening with her on the terrace an hour later, Milton Finigan Hedgewick, Duke of Lamont, enjoyed a quiet reprieve in his bedchamber. Mostly because he needed to clear his head and cool his ardor. *Christ!* He'd never expected to be so physically attracted to her. Nearing his fortieth year and still consumed by anguish, he would have imagined himself incapable of experiencing such bone deep desire, and yet, she'd stirred a thirst in him that would not be easily quenched.

It was unsettling since he doubted she felt the same – that she ever would. The age difference was simply too great. He laughed with misery and tossed back the rest of his brandy. Offering her comfort, a prestigious position, and vast amounts of wealth was one thing. Lusting after her would be entirely different. She was unlikely to welcome it while he…He expelled a tortured breath. If only he were ten years younger. Perhaps then he wouldn't seem quite so old.

Rising, he pulled on his jacket and went to the

door. Maybe he should reconsider his intention to court her. She deserved someone closer to her own age – someone with a happier outlook on life. He, on the other hand, should seek someone else. A widow, perhaps? Reaching the stairs, he paused to consider. No. He'd evaluated every option and decided nobody else would do. Not if he were to think of Beatrice and Gemma and not if he were to marry the woman who drew him in ways no other ever had. His nieces needed a youthful mother with a lively disposition, while he craved her kindness.

With renewed resolve, Milton wound his way through the maze of hallways that would lead him out to the terrace. But the moment he arrived there and found her waiting, her youthful face so open and trusting, his moral compass began to tremble. Would he truly be able to make her happy?

"Your Grace?" She must have seen his hesitation, for her smile began to fade.

"Forgive me." He strode toward her, the heels of his boots sweeping softly against the snow dusting the terrace like confectioner's sugar. Reaching her, he stared at her upturned face, his gaze sliding across her rose-colored lips and up to her liquid-blue eyes. "Perhaps we should take a moment to consider the consequence of keeping each other's company."

She didn't even flinch. Rather, she linked her arm with his and proceeded to walk, leaving him with no other option than to accompany her. "If the lack of a chaperone is your concern, you may rest assured my maid and a footman will be present. They have simply gone ahead in order to set up chairs and blankets for us."

"I should have thought of that."

"They have also prepared the skates. So unless you intend to break your promise to me…"

He drew her to a halt and turned her toward him, his heart thudding against the tightening of his chest. "I would not do so without good reason. It is just…" *Oh hell! He was going to have to be honest.* "My feelings for you are such that it might be best if you kept your distance."

This seemed to confuse her. She considered him from beneath a heavy frown. "Whatever do you mean?"

In all of his eight and thirty years, Milton had never – not once – felt himself blush. How could he possibly tell this innocent creature how much he desired her, of the hunger she instilled in him, that even now as she stood before him covered from head to toe, his fingers itched to rip the clothes from her body? Obviously, he could not.

"I am in need of a wife," he told her bluntly, because really, there was no point in denying the fact. "And I had set my sights on you – hence my reason for seeking your company and wishing to watch you interact with Beatrice and Gemma."

"You were interviewing me?"

"In a manner of speaking." He cleared his throat, uncomfortable with the whole debacle. "But I have since reconsidered."

"You have?" Her voice sounded weak.

"I cannot deny my attraction to you or how well you would suit as a mother for Beatrice and Gemma. You have been on my mind since the first time I met you in London last spring. But I fear it would be selfish of me to pursue you in earnest. You deserve a younger man by your side, not someone you'll eventually have to nurse."

Raising her eyebrows, she addressed him with measured words as she quietly asked, "Are you sickly now?"

"No, but it's a fair guess that half of my life is behind me."

"Perhaps," she agreed. Her eyes rested on his, and then she abruptly turned and resumed walking. "Are you coming?"

Blinking, Milton hurried after her. "My lady, I—"

"Laura, if you please."

The informality shook him to his core. He tested the name, allowing it to slide across his tongue with quiet reverence. "Laura." Quickening his pace, he reached her side and grabbed hold of her arm so he could guide her down the steps toward the lawn below. "Did you not hear what I said?"

"What I heard, Your Grace, is that you wish to court me, but that you're afraid I'll be unhappy if we choose to marry. You think making me your duchess would suit everyone except for me, and so you have decided to spare me. Is that the gist of it?" Reaching a graveled path, they continued toward the lake, where the servants could be seen waiting for them.

"Yes. I suppose it is." He drew her closer, inhaling her scent of jasmine as he did so. It made his senses come alive with a sharp awareness that did little to lessen his interest in her.

"As noble as your concerns may be, I would like the opportunity to make my own choices for my future." She tipped her nose up, her cheeks pink-ing in response to the chilly breeze. "I may not be more than twenty, but I do know my own mind, and although you may wish to convince me that you are an ancient fossil–" He coughed, receiving a frank stare in return. "—with nothing but misery to offer, I disagree."

They arrived at the spot where the chairs had been placed. She took a seat, as did he, his eyes settling on the pair of skates waiting at his feet. Did he really have to do this? Laura certainly wasn't hesitating. She was already strapping one onto her right foot. "How can you so easily dismiss our difference in age?" He reluctantly reached for one of the skates and started putting it on. "It may not be so apparent now, but it will become so as we grow older."

"You assume a great deal, Your Grace."

"Milton." He glanced hastily in her direction before starting on the other skate. "If I am to address you by your Christian name, then you must do the same with me."

"Very well then, Milton." She stood, even as he did his best not to fall apart at the sound of her speaking his name with such care and respect. And then she was suddenly crouched before him, helping him with his skate in an intimate way he ought to prevent but could not bring himself to do. "You have your worries, and I have mine. For one thing, I fear I would not be refined enough. My fingers are always stained by ink. There's really no preventing it, given my passion for writing. And as much as I wish I could talk about politics with you, I fear myself incapable of it. So then, perhaps it is I who should spare you from having to endure a messy simpleton."

He stared at her, dumbfounded by her admission. "You cannot possibly believe such things would bother me."

"Do they not?"

"No." He reached for her hand, turning it over in his while he stared down at the dark blotches marking her skin. "And I would never ask you to give up your writing. Rather, I would encourage it."

The smile she gave him in response was magical. It pulled him to her, so close he could see the deeper shades of violet darkening the edges of her eyes. "Then let us dispense with this conversation and focus on compatibility instead. For one thing," she said, helping him to his feet, "the man I marry must be able to skate."

"Surely you jest?"

A laugh escaped her. "Of course I do." Linking her arm with his, she guided him toward the edge of the lake. "Try to keep your balance as well as possible."

Carefully, he followed her out onto the frozen water, testing his stability as he went, one inch at a time. "I feel like I'm made of wood."

"It takes some getting used to, and fear of falling isn't helping. Do you think you can try to relax?"

He made an effort, but she was right. "Ever since the accident, I've been afraid of things that never worried me before. But if a simple carriage ride could lead to such disaster, then…"

Unwinding her arm from his, she grabbed hold of his hand, comforting him with her touch. "The Countess of Darkhaven fell down a flight of stairs years ago and broke her neck," Laura reminded him. He stumbled a little but managed to regain his balance. "Accidents happen, but if you constantly try to avoid them, you'll find yourself locked up in a room, without courage to venture outside."

She was right. Of course she was. So he swallowed his apprehension and slid one foot forward like her, then the other. "Am I doing this right?"

"You are doing splendidly, Milton."

Her words warmed his heart, encouraging him to continue. And as he eventually grew more confident, accompanying her at a moderate pace, he felt free for the first time since receiving word of his father's and brother's demise. Who knew overcoming an obstacle – of running toward it rather than away – could be so liberating?

"Thank you for this," he called to Laura while they skated past the Endurance. The massive ship was no longer used for sailing but rather for hosting romantic dinners during the warmer seasons of the year.

"You're smiling." Slowing her pace, she eventually pulled him to a halt with her.

"Am I?"

She nodded. "Perhaps you ought to go skating more often."

Staring back into her sparkling eyes, he couldn't help but agree. He glanced around and noticed they were well out of sight from the shore, hidden behind the Endurance's port. It was a rare opportunity – a welcome one. And yet … "We should probably get back."

"Yes." But rather than set off again, she remained where she was, her eyes brimming with the sort of expectancy that was likely to burn right through him.

"If we don't…" She came a bit closer, and he expelled a ragged breath. "You cannot possibly know what you do to me."

Her lips parted ever so slightly before she dared ask, "Will you tell me?"

A rush of air filled his lungs on a sharp inhale. Christ, she was brazen, and he…he was tempted to do things the gentleman in him would never before have allowed. But this was it. She was asking, and so he would tell her and let her run— or skate—as fast away from him as she was able.

"I have never wanted a woman as much as I want you. If we marry, I believe you'll be faced with many sleepless nights since I'll be trying to bed you at every available opportunity." Her eyes had gone wide, no doubt with trepidation, shock, or horror, but he couldn't seem to stop. "You've lit a fire in me that must be fed – a need impossible for me to ignore. I…I fear such a fate will not be to your liking."

"Because there are nearly twenty years between us?" Raising her hand, she set her palm against his cheek. The soft leather of her gloves was cool against his skin. "You think me incapable of sharing your attraction?"

"You cannot possibly."

"So then, you imagined we would enjoy a marriage where I would simply do my duty while you take all the pleasure?"

He was well past his prime and planning to take her to bed, selfish bastard that he was, though he was doing his damnedest not to be. "It wouldn't be right. I am aware." He blew out his breath and pushed his hands through his hair. "I never meant to be quite so drawn to you."

Her mouth dropped open. "That's a bit insulting."

"I didn't mean for it to be." Why couldn't he say the right thing? She tipped her head in expectation. "What I mean is that I thought we might have a companionable relationship, one in which you would be spared from…ahem…having to perform on a…er…regular basis."

Closing her mouth, she allowed a mischievous smile. "Did it ever occur to you I might wish to perform on a regular basis?"

"No. Never." He could barely hold himself upright at the idea she might.

"Perhaps I've had some wild imaginings of my own." She licked her lips. "Maybe you're not the only one who dreams of engaging in passionate bedsport."

"Dear God in heaven!"

Her eyes went wide. "Oh dear. Have I scared you off now?"

"No, Laura. Quite the contrary." And although he felt horribly awkward, poised as he was on a pair of skates, he closed the distance between them and lowered his mouth onto hers. *Yes!* She was warm and welcoming – a perfect treat for him to enjoy – and she was making the most delightful sounds. Sweeping his arms around her, he angled his face and deepened the kiss, tasting her sweetness while savoring the feel of her body pressed against his. She was all pliable curves beneath her pelisse and gown, and he couldn't wait for the chance to unwrap her completely, his breath already heavy with the heat of his desire.

"Christ, Laura, you make me want to claim you right here, right now."

"With the servants waiting on the other side of the ship?" she asked with a giggle.

He kissed his way along her cheek. Reaching her ear, he quietly whispered, "We've been gone for a while now. In their minds the deed has likely been done already." And then, in an act of lust so apart from his otherwise stoic nature, he held her in place and pushed up against her. The sigh she emitted almost undid him, but his purpose kept him on course as he told her severely, "Take a moment to consider if this is what you truly want, Laura, because once I have you, there'll be no going back." Releasing her, he retreated to add an arm's length of distance.

"I—"

"One week to think of your future. On that I must insist." Even though not having her at this point would likely be the death of him, he had to give her this chance for certainty. "If you still want me after that, I shall be yours, as you shall be mine."

He didn't fail to notice the flare of desire that sparked in her eyes as he said it. But he had no illusion it might be brought on by circumstance – a natural reaction to a man's attention and the lust-induced kiss he'd delivered. What he needed was to know she truly felt this strongly for him, that he was the cause of her need and not merely a means by which to sate it.

With this in mind, he held out his hand. She grabbed it with only a small degree of hesitation, not saying a word while she guided him back to shore. And although she kept quiet, he noticed the flush that crept into her cheeks when they eventually parted. He'd affected her, no doubt about it. All he could do now was hope he'd done so enough to convince her a lifetime with him would be filled with immeasurable pleasure.

CHAPTER NINE

Nestling her sketchpad in her lap, Emily stared up at the Carravagio painting that hung on the wall before her. She should have brought a chair, she reflected, or at least a stool to sit on. Instead, her legs were stretched out before her on the cool marble floor, her puffy skirts tucked beneath them. She gazed at the warm display of color. The artist was a master at using light to his advantage, of causing a beam of it to make his subjects glow upon the canvas.

Setting her pencil to the paper, she began from the left with the chair and the man who was seated upon it. Her strokes were light and swift as she moved on to the next individual, marking the spots where each person ought to be placed in relation to the other. Satisfied, she began adding details until faces started to emerge, the pressure of her pencil more deliberate now as she added contours and shadows.

"It's quite the masterpiece, is it not?"

Startled by the masculine tone that had spoken, Emily looked up from her sketchpad to find the Earl of Montsmouth standing off to one side. He wore a bright green velvet jacket and a pair of charcoal-colored trousers that seemed to accentuate his height. His hair reminded Emily of slick raven feathers, the fine bone structure of his face affording him with the predatory look of a fox. She'd always considered him a little peculiar – a man who seemed to prefer his own company to that of others – so it had surprised her when he'd arrived to join the festivities.

"He is one of my favorite artists." Emily hastily turned the page of her sketchpad, hiding it from view.

Slowly, Montsmouth lowered the monocle through which he'd been studying the painting and turned to face her. A flicker of interest appeared in his amber eyes. He considered her for a moment before moving closer, his languid pace disturbing the sense of calm she'd possessed before his arrival. "And you are an artist too." He held out his hand with confident expectation.

Emily shook her head. "No." She hugged the sketchbook against her chest.

An elegant eyebrow drew upward, and he lowered his hand, clasping it with his other behind his back. "Because you're afraid," he pronounced.

"Because I know I'm not good enough," she explained. "I merely dabble, like most young ladies do."

A snort was his first response to her statement, and she dearly wished it would be the end of their discussion – that he would simply move on so she might return to her sketch. Instead, he surprised her by claiming a spot beside her on the floor. "Well, one thing is certain: you can never call yourself an artist until you have the courage to share your work with others."

"I would not wish to trouble any audience with my meager efforts."

"Then why bother at all?"

The question made her turn her head to stare at him. "For my own pleasure, my lord."

He turned his head as well, facing her directly. "Is that satisfying enough for you?"

"I…" She'd never really considered such a question before and could only blink at him now as words failed her.

Nodding, he gave her a knowing smile, one that transformed his features from cool aloofness to pleasant thoughtfulness. "Have I happened upon your secret desire, Lady Emily?"

She stared at him. How could somebody take a mere glance at her and suddenly know her better than she knew herself? It seemed incredible. And yet, she felt her heart flutter with renewed vigor while a dream, somehow buried beneath duty and stricture, rose to the surface and offered an invitation. "For years I've been practicing, improving my skill, but I fear it isn't enough – that it will never be enough."

"So you prefer to remain unheard? Silent? To deny the world your talent?"

"Talent?" she scoffed. "How can you possibly suppose I might have any when you haven't even seen my drawings yet?"

He tilted his head, his eyes fixed on hers as though he were reading her like a book. "I cannot, but the intensity with which you were looking at that painting, picking it apart with your eyes, suggests great passion. This is not born without reason, my lady." He held his hand toward her sketchbook once more. "If I may?"

Feeling as though she stood on a precipice, Emily reluctantly handed it to him. After all, if she could not take the critique of a stranger, then what hope would she have of ever becoming the artist she secretly wished to be? So she watched with her heart in her throat while he carefully opened the book, betraying no hint of opinion when the first images came into view.

"Those were nothing more than a few quick sketches," she explained, in the hope he wouldn't judge her on the unfinished scribbles she'd made on a rainy afternoon when she'd had nothing better to do.

He didn't comment. Instead, he held up his hand, silencing her while his gaze remained fixed on the hurried pencil strokes slashing across the paper. Turning the page, he gave an equal amount of attention to a watercolor portraying a dark alley where a beggar sat, while a wealthy man nearby bargained with a whore. Montsmouth's eyebrows rose a notch, and Emily's heart flipped over.

"That's just—" she began to explain.

"Hush." He silenced her once again.

Swallowing, she instinctively rose, unable to remain by his side while he peered into the private world she'd created for herself. She crossed to the window and looked out at the snow-covered landscape. Far below, she could see Laura and Lamont skating across the lake, while two servants stood in attendance on the embankment. A smile touched Emily's lips when the duke reached out his arms for balance in an effort to follow her sister. The poor man had adamantly declared his disinterest in skating, and yet there he was, doing his best to stay upright.

Unwilling to pry, she turned away from the scene, though she couldn't quite stop from wondering if more Thorncliff romances might be underway. Earlier, she'd seen Rachel smile while she walked with Belgrave, which was most unusual since Rachel rarely found anything amusing. And then there was Fiona and Chadwick. Emily had not been able to keep from noticing the way the two continued to eye each other whenever they were in the same room.

The only eligible gentleman remaining was Montsmouth. Sighing, she glanced across at where he sat, his complete attention riveted on the image of a child clutching his mother as she soothed away his pain. There was little likelihood of her forming an attachment to him, considering how uncomfortable he made her feel. His searching eyes and strange ability to show up when least expected put her on edge in a way she didn't care for in the least. And yet, he seemed transfixed by what he was seeing right now.

Eventually, after another ten minutes had passed and Emily's stomach had twisted itself into such a tight knot she felt she might be sick, he closed the book and stood. "Thank you." He handed it back to her. "I am honored you would trust me with your work."

For the first time, she saw warmth reflected in the depth of his otherwise cool expression. And so she expelled the breath she'd been holding and dared ask, "What do you think of it?"

He studied her for a moment, long enough for fear to creep into her heart and for her to regret ever showing an interest in his opinion. But then a smile touched his lips, and he spoke with the sort of sincerity that could not be fabricated. "You are far more talented than I imagined, Lady Emily. Your ability to capture human emotion is unparalleled."

Unable to speak as she tried to comprehend what he'd told her, she simply stared back. Her silence eventually prompted him to turn away and start walking along the length of the gallery. She blinked, gathered her thoughts, and hastened after him with her sketchbook firmly tucked beneath her arm. "Do you mean it?" she asked, drawing up beside him.

He glanced at her briefly before giving his attention to the paintings they passed on their way. "Do you doubt me?"

"Well, no. Of course not." She feared she might have insulted him now. "But your praise is greater than I anticipated."

He paused in front of an impressive Goya and spoke in an even tone demanding attention. "There are those who visit Thorncliff because they welcome an extravagant retreat. My motive for being here is entirely different. I come for the art." He dropped a look in her direction as if to ensure she was listening. Their eyes met, and she suddenly had the distinct impression her opinion of him as a standoffish dandy was entirely misplaced. "My own private collection is something to be admired. I visit auctions at regular intervals and have dedicated much of my life to studying the masters. If there is one thing I'm capable of recognizing when I see it, it is talent, Lady Emily. Believe me when I tell you that yours should be celebrated. If you wish it, you may become one of the best known artists of our time."

"You flatter me, my lord."

"I only speak the truth," he told her sharply.

She inhaled deeply. "I don't know what to say." Not in a million years would she have guessed how much they had in common – that he was so invested in art. "Perhaps one day you'll invite me to view your collection?"

Her boldness surprised her. She never would have dared to propose such a thing half an hour earlier, but something had changed since then. In the most unlikely way possible, she felt a connection to Montsmouth she'd never had with anyone else before. He'd seen her soul and applauded it. Her head felt light at the very notion.

"It would be my pleasure to do so," he murmured. His tone was deeper than before, conveying a rich, velvety feel that made her skin prick with a new sort of awareness. "And," he added, proceeding along the gallery once more, "if you'll allow it, I will happily help you advance your career. My connections in the art world are numerous."

"Oh!" She felt a broad smile slide into place. Her heart soared with possibilities. "Do you think I might be ready to do so?"

"You are beyond ready, my lady." Halting, he turned to face her with penetrating eyes. "I suggest we take a few of your sketches to crop and frame. In my opinion they will do splendidly in a private event sale – at least twelve pounds apiece, I should think."

"That's quite…er…" She took a moment to steady her anxious nerves. "Unexpected."

"Now, you have to understand there are no guarantees, but I am optimistic where you are concerned, and I say that with the greatest respect."

"You said you came here for the art." For reasons she couldn't quite understand, she felt a need to know more about him now – to understand the person he was, since he obviously wasn't at all the man she'd assumed him to be. "Is that why you've be roaming the estate during your visits?" When he failed to answer, she added, "When I was last here during the summer, I got the distinct impression you were searching all of the rooms. I suppose that makes sense if you were hunting for paintings."

"I was certainly doing that." They'd reached the door at the end of the gallery. His hand reached for the handle, allowing it to swing open. "After you, my lady."

Something in his voice suggested there was more to his interest in Thorncliff than a simple fondness for art. She pondered this notion as she preceded him into the hallway beyond. Stopping there while he closed the door behind them, she chose to sate her curiosity by candidly asking, "What exactly do you mean?"

For a second, it seemed he would tell her, but then his gaze shuttered and he turned away, heading in the direction of the stairs. "I believe I'll go and rest for a while before supper." Swiveling on his heels, he reached for her hand while executing a flamboyant bow. His lips grazed her knuckles for the briefest of seconds – long enough for her heart to flutter – before he straightened and took a step back. "If you'll please excuse me?"

With her thoughts and emotions in complete disarray, Emily managed a hasty nod. "Of course. I'll look forward to seeing you later."

He dipped his head in response, allowed a slight smile, and then he was gone, up the stairs to his chamber. Emily stared at the spot where he'd stood seconds before, more confused than she'd ever felt in her life, not just by the man, but by the startling realization she might be developing feelings for him.

CHAPTER TEN

A CLOCK IN THE HALL CHIMED the hour – two in the morning – as Charles Augustus Reeves, Earl of Montsmouth, made his way through the darkness. Supper had been delicious, as usual, though he wished he'd been seated closer to Lady Emily. Something about her kept his mind fixed upon her person. It was unrelenting. As hard as he'd tried to push her from his thoughts and focus on his task, the lady made him long for more than he could allow himself at present. She was a distraction, an unwelcome one considering his purpose at Thorncliff, but he'd been honest about her talent. It was both admirable and, for a man with an insatiable appetite for art, incredibly tempting.

Turning a corner, he paused to listen, ensuring nobody else was around before continuing on his way. He'd deliberately dimmed the light of the lantern he carried as much as possible so as not to draw attention from any lingering servants. To his relief, it did appear as though everyone had retired, which meant the house was his, ready to be explored.

So he made his way toward the interior courtyard. When he'd last been here, the steps from there leading into the hallways below had been frequently used by Mr. Heartly and Mary Bourneville, now Mrs. Heartly. They'd made it impossible for Charles to venture below stairs in private or without the risk of discovery. He would do so now and, hopefully, find the reward he sought. Because he was fairly certain it wasn't hidden on the ground floor. He'd searched every room there during the summer, including the conservatory.

But as he neared the door to the stairwell, he sensed another presence in the courtyard and quickly turned, scanning the space while keeping close to the shadowy corner. A movement off to one side caught his attention, and he was finally sure he'd been spotted.

"Who goes there?" he asked the murky shades.

At the sound of a sharp inhale, he immediately turned up the light, holding his lantern high in order to push back the colors of night. She stepped into the yellow glow with a hesitant tread that lent an ethereal quality to her poise. "Lady Emily?"

For a second, he thought she might be a dream brought to life by his recent ponderings of her. Certainly, she was a vision with her silky robe cinched at her waist, the fabric flowing around her figure like mist across the moors. He shook his head and addressed her more firmly. "What are you doing here?"

"I might ask the same of you," she said.

Another step, and she was close enough to touch. Dressed as she was, it was going to be difficult for him not to. He tried instead to offer a convincing answer. "I couldn't sleep so I chose to go for a stroll."

"Me too." Her lips, he saw, hinted at a smile.

"You're being deceptive."

"No more than you."

Her frankness caught him off guard. He held the light closer to her face, studying her expression while assessing her possible motive. Eventually, he was forced to ask, "Have you been following me?"

"No. I was in the parlor working on one of my sketches."

"Why not do so in your chamber? Why the need to come downstairs in…" *such a state of undress* "… the middle of the night?"

She shrugged one shoulder. "I decided to have a glass of sherry to help me rest."

"I see." He could think of nothing else to say at present.

"After turning off the light with the intention of retiring," she continued, "I exited the room and saw you wandering about in the dark."

"Why didn't you say something?"

"Because I didn't know if it was you at first, and because I was curious to see what was going on. People don't usually wander about houses in the dark for no good reason. Naturally, I'm now quite convinced you must be up to something, Lord Montsmouth. The only question is what."

Grinding his teeth, Charles stared back at the woman before him. The determined glint in her eyes told him she would not be easily dismissed with a lie. Still, he wasn't sure if he could trust her with the truth. After all, she seemed like an honorable creature who'd likely brand him a thief if she truly knew what he planned. *Christ!* He should have been more careful, should not have engaged her in conversation earlier. Because then he might not have cared about being a cad, of putting himself before her. Now, however, after she'd trusted him with her heart and her soul, allowed him to judge both, he felt compelled to give her nothing but sincerity in return.

"Very well," he found himself saying, "come with me, and I shall tell you."

She followed him into the nearest room. It was one of the themed salons – the Greek one, with columns and marble sculptures of deities scattered throughout. The furniture stood like forgotten memories covered in white cotton sheets. With no fire present, it was cooler than the more frequented parts of the house. Closing the door, Charles turned to face Lady Emily and reflexively drew a sharp breath as he drank in her figure. She was stunning – slender with curves that begged for a man to explore her. A temptress, with her brown hair undone in a river of curls tumbling over her shoulders.

Flexing his fingers, Charles fought the urge to step toward her and run his hands through the silky tresses. Instead, he made a valiant attempt to focus on the matter at hand. "What I'm about to tell you will require your complete discretion." When all she did was nod, he forced his most serious tone and asked, "Can I trust you?"

"Of course, my lord. You have my word." Her soft spoken words were followed by a distinct shudder.

"You are cold." He should have taken her to the parlor. It was probably warmer there, even if the fire had already been extinguished. Regretting his insensitivity, he shrugged out of his jacket and went to give it to her. She took a step back. "My lady, I only mean to offer some means of comfort. If you will permit?"

She gave him a wary look for which he could not fault her. After all, he'd lured her into a room in the middle of the night and shut the door firmly behind them. For all she knew, he meant to be anything but a gentleman now.

He moved toward her with hesitant steps.

Bravely, she remained where she was, though her sharp inhale of breath was not lost on him as he settled the jacket over her shoulders. Her hair caught on the collar, and he could no longer help it. With rigid fingers, he allowed himself the pleasure of pulling it free, of letting it slide across his skin in a gentle caress that set his soul on fire. God help him, he wanted this woman, her passion for art and her unearthly beauty calling for him to adore her.

Trembling with the effort it took him to bank his most carnal desires, he took a step back and exhaled, though not before noting how still she'd gone or how shallow her breaths had become. Perhaps she was not unaffected by his nearness? No. Of course she wasn't. He'd seen apprehension lighting her eyes not only here but when he'd approached her earlier in the gallery as well. She didn't feel comfortable in his presence, that much was certain. And since he was not in the habit of playing the scoundrel, he retreated, adding distance.

"Better?" he asked.

"Yes." She nodded, and her entire posture eased

as if with relief. "Thank you."

Determined not to take offense or submit to the pang of pain that shot through his chest in response to her obvious reluctance to having him near her, he chose to address his reason for walking the halls late at night. "Are you familiar with the rumors regarding a treasure that's supposedly hidden away here on the estate?"

She stared at him with wide eyes. Her lips parted ever so slightly. A second passed before she seemed to collect herself and offer confirmation in the form of a nod. "Yes. Of course I am."

"Lady Duncaster insists there's nothing to it, that she would have found it herself if it truly existed."

"But you believe otherwise?" Her expression was one of intense curiosity now.

He tilted his head. "You don't sound surprised."

"Perhaps I'm not."

This caught his attention. "Why?"

Her tongue darted out, licking her lips as she stared straight back at his eyes. Charles felt his chest tighten. He struggled for air, his feet firmly planted upon the marble floor, willing himself to remain where he was. To his utter consternation, she moved toward him instead, forcing his heartbeat into a rapid gallop while heat flooded his limbs. Curling his fingers into fists, he strained against the urge to pull her into his arms and kiss her until she could barely recall her own name. God! What the hell was he thinking?

"My sister Fiona is convinced the treasure is here as well," Lady Emily said. She spoke with a frankness that pulled him out of the tortured state he was in and forced him to think of the reason he'd come here in the first place. "She has been searching for a jewelry box that used to belong to our grandmother's sister, the Duchess of Marveille. She was French – guillotined during the Revolution."

"I'm sorry. I never realized."

"My grandmother never recovered from the news of it. She wrote in her journal that her sister sent her a box before her death. While we were here for the summer, my brother Richard found a letter referencing it. The description was accurate, and from what I understand, Grandpapa came here to collect it. But upon his arrival at Thorncliff, something must have gone wrong, because both men left with haste as if fleeing a threat and succumbed to the sea on their way back toward France."

"So the box was never recovered?"

She shook her head. "No."

Filing away this bit of information, he carefully asked, "The letter you mentioned. Where did your brother find it?"

"I've been sworn to silence about it."

His eyebrows shot up with surprise. "Really?" This could only mean one thing – the Heartlys had found something, and they meant to hide it. "And Lady Duncaster?"

"She is the one who insisted on keeping all the information we uncovered secret."

"You mean there's more?" When she gave him a blank stare, he failed to keep his irritation at bay, and he told her sharply, "You said *all* the information, Lady Emily."

"I'm sorry, but I cannot betray Lady Duncaster's trust."

"Not even if I were to tell you of my own connection to the treasure?" He saw the flicker of uncertainty in her eyes, fleeting though it was. "Perhaps if we work together, we'll actually manage to find it."

"My siblings made a thorough search of the estate when they were last here and—"

"There's more than your grandmother's jewelry box, my lady. There is art and literature – knowledge that may remain hidden forever unless we manage to find it."

She stared at him with incomprehension until she suddenly blinked and quietly asked, "How can you possibly know this?"

"Because my grandfather told me about it on his death bed. He…" Charles drew a shuddering breath and thought back on that conversation. "I know he was old and not quite in his right mind toward the end, but he was adamant about having collaborated with the previous Earl of Duncaster and two others whose names he never mentioned. He kept saying he'd helped to free his French brothers and sisters and to protect their most prized possessions from falling into the wrong hands. The way he spoke… It was a confession."

"How so?"

"Because he kept asking for forgiveness, insisting his betrayal had cost more than he'd ever intended." Her shocked expression forced Charles to move on quickly, to change the subject so she would not judge him by association. "Finally, before he drew his last breath, he told me all of these valuables he and others had retrieved were enshrined within Thorncliff itself. He spoke cryptically but with conviction. I cannot think he tried to fool me."

"No. I don't believe he did." Hugging herself, she moved between the furniture until she reached a sofa. Lowering herself to it, she stared out over an invisible horizon before turning her gaze back toward him. "Does the North, South, East, or West Wind mean anything to you?"

Charles felt his heart thud against his chest in a dull monotonous motion. "Yes. Grandpapa kept saying the wind blows from the north. It made no sense to me at the time. I always assumed it was a sign of death creeping in."

Silence sank between them, and for a long moment, she stared back at him from her position on the sofa. "What I believe, based on what you've told me, is that your grandfather was one of the Cardinals."

Confused, he shook his head. "No. He was a peer with little connection to the church and certainly not a Catholic."

A sympathetic smile touched Lady Emily's lips. "What I speak of has nothing to do with religion, but with a group of three men and one woman – liberators who fought for the French aristocracy during a terrible time in its history. Aside from your grandfather, they consisted of Lord Duncaster, the Duchess of Marveille, and my grandfather, the previous Earl of Oakland."

"How do you know so much about all of this?"

"I didn't until recently. But when Spencer's wife found my greataunt's earring in an underground passageway leading to the sea, and Richard uncovered a Roman villa beneath Thorncliff along with the letter I mentioned before, and my sister Chloe and her husband helped bring down the Electors, they saw that everything was connected. With Lady Duncaster's permission, they shared what they knew with the rest of us."

"But the jewelry box and the treasure remain hidden."

"Yes. Fiona is still determined to find them, though the rest of us have pretty much given up hope of ever doing so."

He stared at her with incredulity. "I can't believe there's a Roman villa beneath Thorncliff."

"Nor could I until I saw it with my own eyes. It seems to have been used as the Cardinals' headquarters."

"Jesus." The amount of information she'd given him was staggering. He was having some difficulty processing it all and everything it implied. "These Electors you mention, do you know who they are?"

"Of course. They were brought to justice by my brother-in-law, the Duke of Stonegate. As I recall, his guardian, the Marquess of Hainsworth, turned out to be the leader of the Electors – a criminal mastermind by all accounts."

Her words almost caused Charles to stagger. Reaching out, he steadied himself against the edge of a nearby table. "I think I need a drink."

"You do look rather pale."

"That's because…" Oh dear God, how was he to tell her? "Hainsworth visited my grandfather on a regular basis. The two were close friends and… when he attended my grandfather's funeral and offered his condolences, I recall him saying my grandfather had been a trusted ally – a man on whom he'd been able to depend. He told me he'd always helped him fight his adversaries, but I never imagined…I believed he referred to opposing investors or some such thing. Now, after everything you've told me, I think it's clear to assume—"

"Your grandfather was the spy who betrayed them all."

Her words, a mere whisper, hit him like a blow. To think he was related to a man who'd acted so selfishly – so dishonorably – was beyond the pale. He could not stand the idea of sharing his blood, of actually having mourned his loss.

"I'm sorry." The words would not suffice. Nothing would. And she, the lady who'd captured his every awareness, would no longer look at him without knowing what he'd come from. It disgusted him to his core that she should be made aware of such a blemish upon his name.

"What for?" She stood and moved toward him, her face illuminating with a faint yellow glow when she stepped further into the light. "You had nothing to do with it, and you were not there to decide your grandfather's actions."

"But I—"

"No." Her voice was soft but firm. "Any guilt on your part is unfounded. Release yourself from it, Lord Montsmouth."

"How can you be so forgiving?"

"Because there is nothing for me to forgive." She came to a halt immediately before him, and her eyes met his once more before she glanced toward the door. "Shall we look for that drink you mentioned?"

She was close, so close he could see her pulse

pushing against the side of her neck – and he could not stop himself any longer. He reached out, his hand brushing hers, and while he half expected her to pull away, half hoped she would do so in fact, she remained where she was while their fingers continued to touch.

A surge of warmth filled his chest at the scarce bit of intimate contact, and his mind was infused with an endless selection of possibilities. He chose to pick the first, his hand closing over hers and pulling her to him. The gasp that spilled from her lips was enough to drive his cravings to the brink of insanity, but the feel of her suppleness pressed against him, the curve of her back as he reached round to hold her, made him want far more than he'd ever deserve.

"You enchant me," he murmured, dipping his head toward hers and capturing her mouth in a reverent kiss that did nothing to cool his ardor. Hell, not even the chilly room could make him feel anything other than scorched. And the tiny murmur of pleasure that rose from her throat when he deepened the kiss and tightened his hold was delicious in its simplicity, its honesty. God! How the hell had it taken him so long to notice her beauty? And the way she tasted – like the sweetest nectar for him to savor.

"You're divine," he whispered against the cool smoothness of her cheek while he kissed his way toward her neck. She smelled like honey and lemon, perhaps with a hint of jasmine. Incredible, but an innocent he would do well to respect.

So he drew back gently, tucked one of her stray curls behind her ear, and spoke with his heart. "I hope your lack of retreat conveys your agreement to let me court you?"

The smile she offered in return was dazzling indeed. "Oh yes. With the greatest of pleasure, my lord."

"Charles, if you please."

Her eyes shone like diamonds. "Very well, then." She inhaled the air and expelled it again with his name. "Charles."

CHAPTER ELEVEN

REACHING FOR HER TEACUP, FIONA took a sip of the soothing brew it contained while considering all that had happened during the few short days since her arrival at Thorncliff. Seated in the green salon, she'd chosen to spend the afternoon with her sisters. Hopefully, she'd be able to focus on something besides Chadwick and her strange new feelings for him. The man was proving to be a terrible distraction, even if he had agreed to help her search for the treasure.

Determined not to think of him any longer or the odd effect he was having on her, she set her cup aside and said, "So? What have you all been doing for the last few days? I feel as though I've scarcely seen you at all."

"Well..." Rachel sat as stiff as a fence pole, her face more flushed than usual. It hadn't escaped Fiona that she'd been making a bit more effort with her hair styles lately, though her choice of clothing remained the same. "I've been studying a few books from the library."

She fidgeted slightly, and Fiona narrowed her

eyes. "Is it my imagination, or are your nerves all jumbled up?"

"I don't know what you mean."

"Fiona's right," Laura said. "You always appear to be perfectly poised with a cool demeanor that might be mistaken for indifference. Naturally, we're curious to know the cause of this sudden change in you." She allowed a secretive smile before leaning forward and whispering, "Might it have something to do with Lord Belgrave?"

Rachel's eyes widened, and she suddenly turned the color of a beetroot. "He has proven to be quite an engaging conversationalist."

A cheeky smile spread across Emily's lips. "You *like* him!"

"Of course I do. He's perfectly cordial."

Fiona couldn't quite keep back the snicker that bubbled inside her. It burst from her with a snort. "Cordial?" She shook her head in amusement. "Only you would think to describe a gentleman you admire as cordial."

"I'd say he's rather attractive," Laura murmured.

"More so than Lamont?" Emily asked, and it was Laura's turn to blush. "I saw the two of you skating out on the lake yesterday."

Averting her gaze, Laura spoke to the carpet. "He's a man touched by tragedy, but beneath the pain, there's a heart yearning to be cherished."

"And would you like to be the one to cherish it?" Emily asked.

"Well I…I don't really…" Laura finished her incomplete sentence with a shrug.

"He does seem awfully grave," Fiona said, "though that probably appeals to your romantic nature. But what about his age?"

Laura's head snapped up, her eyes suddenly flashing with intensity. She stared back at Fiona with uncharacteristic fierceness. "What of it?" she challenged.

"Well…" Sensing her sister's defensiveness, Fiona wasn't sure whether to drop the issue or press it, on account of having Laura's best interests in mind.

"He is almost twenty years your senior," Rachel pointed out with her usual use of the facts.

Laura rewarded her comment with a glare. "Yes. He is." She looked at her other two sisters. "Does that mean he's undeserving of my attention? Of my affection?"

"No," Emily told her calmly. "We only mean to caution you dear, to ensure you have thought the matter through before things escalate between you."

"The difference in age might not be so great now," Rachel said, "but as you grow older, that can change."

"You worry I shall be a young wife with an ailing husband?" Laura's voice held an element of steel to it. "There are plenty of women who choose to marry older husbands for far more callous reasons than I would ever do."

"You really care for him," Fiona said, a little surprised by this sudden attachment.

"I will say my affections for him have increased significantly since spending more time in his company," Laura admitted. "And I have met his charges as well. Both are tremendously delightful and not the least bit standoffish, as one might have expected them to be."

"Has he proposed courtship then?" Emily asked.

Laura's eyes lit with a sparkle that answered all of their questions before she managed a proper reply. "He has made his intentions known. And I…" Her cheeks seemed to bloom like magnolia petals unfurling in the spring. "I have never been so happy in all of my life."

"Then we are happy for you," Fiona said, while her own heart ached with a strange little pang. She pushed the unpleasant feeling aside and smiled at her sister. "For you to find love, Laura—"

"Oh, it is too soon to say I achieved that much, but I must admit I am greatly encouraged by His Grace's attentions." Pausing, she considered Rachel for a moment before saying, "Perhaps we will both leave here with fiancés?"

"Oh!" Rachel eyed them all in turn before quietly shaking her head. "I'm not sure I'd go quite that far."

"Your blush says otherwise," Fiona murmured.

Rachel pressed her lips together for a moment before saying, "I consider Belgrave a friend, Fiona. To presume he is more than that…that he would ever…" She puffed out a breath. "Well, it would be highly unlikely."

"So the only issue here is that you think yourself unworthy," Emily told her.

"No." Rachel reached for her teacup, the piece of china rattling ever so slightly against her saucer as she did so. "It isn't so simple at all."

"Really?" Laura sounded as dubious as Fiona felt. "We could help you feel more…desirable, if that is what you would like?"

Rachel's mouth dropped open. "How can you

possibly think like that?"

A crease formed above Laura's nose. "I think most young ladies do." She bit her lip and fell silent.

"Laura's right," Fiona said, deciding to jump in and help Rachel out. It was obvious she wanted Belgrave to find her attractive, even if she lacked the security to voice or even to think such a thing. "It won't take much effort, but if you truly like Lord Belgrave, there's no shame in making more of an effort for him. As it is, you've already started styling your hair differently in the evenings." Rachel opened her mouth to speak, but Fiona pressed on by adding, "I think it looks really pretty."

"You do?" Rachel couldn't hide her surprise.

"Absolutely," Fiona assured her. Laura and Emily both nodded in agreement.

"All we need to do now is find some different dresses for you. We can ask a maid to alter a few of your own, but other than that, I do think you're Laura's size, so perhaps you can borrow a couple of hers?"

"I couldn't possibly," Rachel protested.

"On the contrary," Laura told her, "I am more than happy to help. Especially if it means facilitating a love match."

"Oh, but I—"

"You'll see," Laura said without blinking an eye. "You'll marry Belgrave. Mark my word."

"And you'll no doubt marry Lamont," Emily said.

Laura beamed with pleasure. She looked from Emily to Fiona and back again. "Which leaves us with the two of you to consider. Don't think I haven't noticed the way you've been looking at

Chadwick, Fiona."

"You've also been keeping each other's company a great deal," Rachel pointed out.

Fiona frowned and shook her head. "We've always enjoyed spending time together."

"Yes," Emily agreed. "But there's something different now. When I saw the two of you talking at breakfast this morning, it was as though you couldn't decide whether or not to flee the room or jump into his lap."

"Don't be absurd!"

He'd been telling her about a ridiculous accident he'd had years ago when he'd been chasing his cousin with a teacup filled with water. He'd meant to toss the water after her, but when he'd done so, the cup had detached from the handle, hurled through the air, and hit his cousin in the back of the head.

Fiona had laughed in an effort to hide her desire to kiss him. It was an urge that had become increasingly prevalent since he'd pressed her into the ground in the forest. Dear God, she could still feel the strength of his pure masculinity burning straight through her whenever she recalled the moment.

Gathering her wits to the best of her ability, she quietly said, "He and I are friends. Nothing more."

"You're being dishonest," Laura told her.

"No. I'm—"

"I saw the way the two of you interacted with each other in the woods when we went to cut pine for the decorations," Rachel said.

Fiddlesticks.

There was no getting past Rachel's observational

nature. Still… "We were playing hide- and-go-seek between the trees."

Emily coughed. "Is that what they call it these days?"

Feeling her skin heat, Fiona crossed her arms and sat back. "He was teasing me, and I ended up tossing a pile of snowballs at him in retaliation. There's nothing wrong with that, even if you're trying to imply otherwise."

Laura rolled her eyes. "What we're implying is, you're no longer a child but a fully grown woman with the means to attract any man of your choosing while he—"

"Is like a brother," Fiona finished, even though she knew her words were a lie. Since returning to Thorncliff and seeing Chadwick again, her thoughts of him had been anything but chaste.

"If you say so," Emily murmured, "though you probably ought to know there is nothing brotherly about the way he's been looking at you."

"Really?" Her sister's words made her stomach feel as though it was turning over.

"It's my opinion," Emily added, "that he is yours if you want him."

"I quite agree," Rachel remarked.

"Me too," Laura said.

Unwilling to linger on the subject any further since she had no wish to succumb to the wave of relief crashing through her or all of the silly feelings it carried with it, Fiona looked at Emily and quietly said, "That leaves you. Unless, of course…" No. It couldn't possibly be, could it? "What is your opinion of the Earl of Montsmouth?"

Emily's change in hue spoke volumes. "I find

him to be far more likeable than I would have imagined."

Silence fell upon them until Laura suddenly drew a sharp breath, expelling it with an avid, "You can't be serious?"

"And why would that be?" Emily asked.

"Because he's an arrogant fop with a degree of social awkwardness that doesn't align with your welcoming nature." Laura shook her head. "I don't see the two of you forming an attachment."

"Well, then, you'll probably be shocked to know we already have."

This news surprised even Fiona. "Really?"

Emily nodded. "He kissed me." She bit her bottom lip as if to stop from smiling like a love-struck fool.

"When?" This question was asked in unison by all three sisters, who each edged forward in their seats.

"Last night. In the Greek salon." She waved away the next question that formed on Fiona's lips. "Don't ask me why we were there for it's a longer story, but it did end with me stepping into his arms and... Oh, it was the most wonderful thing I've ever experienced."

"I must confess, I've always thought the act rather disgusting," Rachel said. "This joining of mouths cannot possibly be healthy."

"Just wait until Belgrave delivers his first kiss to you," Laura said. "I think you'll have a different opinion then."

"You speak as though from experience," Fiona said, not missing the dreamy sigh that had followed Laura's comment.

Laura hesitated briefly before saying, "Well...if you must know, Lamont kissed me as well. When we were out skating there was a moment behind the Endurance, and well, I have to agree with Emily. Kissing is a wonderful thing."

The two sisters shared a secretive smile that Fiona could not quite relate to. Yes, she'd thought of possibly kissing Chadwick and what that might be like, but for the act to leave her looking as giddy as her sisters did right now was highly unlikely. "Will you tell us what it is about Montsmouth that you find so appealing?" she asked in an effort to stay on point.

Emily nodded. "As it turns out, we share an enthusiasm for art. He's quite the collector, and his knowledge is vast. He has even suggested helping me set up an art exhibit of my own."

"So he has actually seen your sketches?" Rachel asked.

"You won't even let us see them," Laura said.

"Only because I never believed them to be good enough," Emily confessed, "but Montsmouth convinced me to be brave. He is incredibly supportive and sincere in his compliments. I cannot help but admire such traits."

"Then I am pleased on your behalf," Fiona told her.

"Plus, he took the courage to place his trust in me." Folding her hands in her lap, she looked at them each in turn before saying, "There is something about him you should know – something he has permitted me to divulge since doing so will be to all of our benefits."

"And what is that?" Fiona asked, unable to

fathom that any of Montsmouth's secrets might interest her.

"Well…" Emily stalled while she took a sip of her tea, returning the cup to its saucer before saying, "Apparently, his grandfather was the fourth Cardinal – the one we've been wondering about."

Air rushed from Fiona's lungs in a moment of disbelief. "Really?"

Emily nodded. "Montsmouth told me there's a great deal more than the jewelry box to be found. There are vast amounts of paintings and books, all saved from the French aristocracy and put into safekeeping here somewhere."

Fiona was so astounded by this new revelation she could scarcely think. "Did he offer any other new information? Any clues as to where it might be hidden?"

"I'm afraid not, but apparently finding it has been his main incentive for coming to Thorncliff."

"Until he met you," Laura said. She gave Emily a nudge.

"Well, the two of us do get on with each other, although I have no illusion of being as important as this hunt he's on. But I do suspect offering to help him with it has endeared me to him tremendously."

Fiona sighed. "Are you certain you wouldn't prefer a different match?"

"To pick a man because there is nobody else is unwise," Rachel said. "After all, you still have one more season at your disposal while I must act while I can if I am to have any hope of marrying."

"You sound as though you're picking Belgrave on the basis of practicality alone," Laura chastised.

"No. There is more to it than that," Rachel said. "Of course there is, or I would not think of it at all. Don't forget I was fully intent on becoming a spinster with no other passion in my life besides science and mathematics. But my perspective has been altered since arriving here. Belgrave…" She dropped her gaze and appeared uncharacteristically confused. "He incites a reaction within me, much like a fire might cause a pot of water to boil. And as strange and peculiar as it is, I find myself wanting more."

Reaching out, Emily pressed her hand against Rachel's and smiled. "I know completely how you feel and I…*we*," she amended with a nod toward Laura and Fiona, "couldn't be happier for you. All I ask is for you to be equally happy for me, because frankly, my heart has been captured by Montsmouth. There's really no going back."

"You have my blessing," Fiona said. She couldn't imagine what their parents might have to say on the matter, but Montsmouth was an earl, which was sure to make up for his peculiar personality. And as long as Emily was happy with him, Fiona couldn't think of their parents objecting.

As for Chadwick… Already she longed to be back in his company. Was it truly possible that he might view her as a potential candidate for wife? Did she even have the courage to explore such a possibility when she couldn't be sure of where her hopes ended and the truth began? What she knew now with conviction was that she longed to experience the joy that shone in both Emily's and Laura's eyes – she longed to be kissed – and she longed for Chadwick to be the man who did so.

CHAPTER TWELVE

THERE WERE THREE CARDS LEFT in his hand. Edward considered the nine of clubs – something small to give Belgrave a chance. Montsmouth threw down a four which Belgrave followed with a six, allowing Lamont to take the trick with the queen.

Blast!

They played the last couple of hands in swift succession with Montsmouth and Lamont pronounced the victors. Edward gathered the cards and returned them to their box. "Good game, gentlemen."

"Indeed." Lamont stood and went to the sideboard. "Perhaps you'll allow me to buy you a drink to make up for your loss?" He gestured toward the selection of carafes.

Edward grinned. "You seem to be in an unusually good mood, Your Grace." He rose from the table, as did Belgrave and Montsmouth. "I'll have a brandy."

"So will I," Belgrave said. Montsmouth seconded the choice, and the three of them crossed to the nearest seating arrangement. "Chadwick's right," the viscount added. He glanced at Lamont, who approached with four glasses balanced on a tray. "There's a definite smile upon your lips. You've even got dimples!"

Lamont immediately frowned, all hints of amusement vanishing from his expression. He quietly set the tray down on the table between them. "Perhaps I'm happy to be here. It's good to get away from home on occasion and simply relax in the company of friends."

"I'll drink to that." Montsmouth raised his glass in salute. Belgrave, Edward, and Lamont followed suit.

"Yes," Edward agreed, "but you didn't appear so when you were here for the summer. Something's different now. A change has come over you during the last few days."

Pressing his lips together, Lamont looked at each of his friends. "Very well, I'll relent, but only if you swear to keep it a secret. For now."

"Of course," Belgrave said.

"You have our word," Montsmouth added.

Edward nodded his agreement, wondering what might have happened to lift the duke's spirits with such swift efficiency. He took another sip of his brandy and watched the duke expectantly.

"I am...enamored," Lamont confessed.

Edward almost spat out his drink. Instead, he managed to clamp his mouth shut, keeping the liquid inside and almost choking on it as a result. Coughing, he couldn't help but notice the looks of surprise on Belgrave's and Montsmouth's' faces. "Enamored?" Edward sputtered. *This*, he had not expected.

"With Lady Laura," Lamont clarified. "She is…" His eyes took on a distant glow. "…quite remarkable."

A moment of silence passed while Edward, Belgrave, and Montsmouth simply stared at Lamont as though seeing the man for the first time. Montsmouth was the first to find his tongue. "Good for you," he said. "You deserve to be happy."

"I'd say we all deserve to be," Lamont murmured.

"Perhaps," Montsmouth acquiesced.

"Judging from your inability to stop from smiling," Edward said, "I presume the lady reciprocates your affection?"

Lamont nodded. "She does indeed. But…" His smile faltered. "Given the circumstances, I have asked her to take a week to consider her options."

Belgrave frowned. "What circumstances?"

"Our difference in age," Lamont said.

He finally looked as grave as Edward was accustomed to him doing, but the expression no longer suited him, and Edward wondered if it ever had. "Age is irrelevant if you care for each other," he told the duke.

"But—"

"The heart wants what the heart wants. If hers is already engaged, then a week of thinking is not going to change that. I should know." He hadn't meant for the last bit to slip out, but there was no taking it back now.

"How do you mean?" Belgrave asked.

Everyone's attention was now riveted on Edward. *Damn it.* He was either going to have to talk or endure an infinite amount of questions. "I've tried to fall out of love. It doesn't work."

"You're in love?" Lamont asked with wide-eyed amazement.

"Did you not think me capable of such profound feeling?" Edward leaned back, stretched out his legs, and crossed his arms. "I know I'm often considered flip, always making jokes and enjoying a good laugh. People don't expect me to think of settling down, taking responsibility, and starting a family. However, when it comes to my estate, I am most dedicated. It's been prosperous ever since I inherited it. There are no debts to speak of."

"Frankly, I've never really wondered about your business acumen," Belgrave said. "But I've only ever known you socially, at parties and such. It makes sense that you might be completely different when dealing with your private affairs."

"I will say, I am lucky to still have my father. He has taught me a great deal and has saved me from carrying your burden, Lamont. And yours, Montsmouth."

Montsmouth dipped his head in acknowledgement. "Not having a father can be quite difficult, but tell me, for it seems as though we've gotten away from it, and my curiosity must be sated. Who is it you pine for?"

"Can you not guess?" Belgrave asked. "It must be Lady Fiona."

"Ah yes," Lamont said. His gaze met Edward's. "Of course."

Expelling a breath, Edward raised his glass to his lips and allowed the spicy liquid to fill his mouth before sliding down his throat, enjoying the way it heated his insides. "Her family and mine have been close for years. I spent many summers at the

Oakland estate and developed a bond that can never be severed. In age, I was closest to Spencer. He and I were at school together, but Lady Fiona was the little sprite who invariably called to the mischief-maker inside me. She was a good sport, always ready for a bit of adventure, so in spite the difference in age, I couldn't help but look forward to seeing her — especially as she got older."

"She is nineteen?" Montsmouth asked.

Edward nodded. "Yes. And I am thirty." He pushed out a breath before saying, "It never feels like much of a gap when I am with her, but on paper, she's a great deal younger than I."

"You're saying this to a man who hopes to marry a woman who's eighteen years his junior," Lamont murmured.

"Quite right," Edward said. He sympathized with the duke and was glad to know there were only eleven years between himself and Fiona. "But it is the reason for my attempts to stay away from the family since the summer. Being near her has become...difficult."

"She doesn't share your sentiment?" Belgrave asked.

"She doesn't know of it."

"Good God, man! Why not?"

"Because once I tell her, there'll be no taking it back. It will alter everything between us and I...I fear losing her friendship over it."

"Then you have no reason to suppose she might feel as strongly for you as you do for her?" Montsmouth asked.

"No. I do not." Edward had done his best to study her expressions whenever they'd been together, but even as he'd pushed her down into the snow and desire had torn through his veins, she'd stared back up at him with bewilderment in her eyes. He could not allow himself to take advantage or to possibly ruin what was between them. "She is young. I dare say she's not yet aware of how easily she can affect a man."

"Perhaps you should simply court her without her being made aware," Belgrave suggested.

Edward frowned. "You want me to trick her?"

"No. Don't be absurd." Belgrave pressed his lips together before clarifying. "Try treating her as a gentleman ought to treat a lady in whom he holds an interest. Take her for strolls, a ride in a carriage, allow the occasional touch and meeting of the eyes. Give her the chance to become more aware of you, a chance for her to change her opinion of you from a brother figure to that of a man she might actually want."

"It's not a bad idea," Lamont said.

"Perhaps not," Edward agreed.

He'd been unable to find the balance between playing the prankster with her and actually being the man whose desire for her would likely lead to his downfall. Perhaps a secret courtship would be the answer. It would, hopefully, give her a means by which to recognize she was now fully grown and that their relationship had to change, one way or the other. They would either succumb to a mutual passion or find a more socially acceptable means of interacting in the future. Naturally, he hoped it might be the former rather than the latter.

"But enough about me," he said, turning his attention on Belgrave and Montsmouth. "Will the two of you tell us how things are progressing with Lady Rachel and Lady Emily?"

"I say," Lamont pronounced, "I wasn't aware there was an interest there."

"On the contrary, my interest in Lady Emily is very sincere," Montsmouth said. His eyes, which were generally cool, had warmed at the mere mention of her name. "I have recently discovered we share an interest in art. She has talent unlike anything else I've ever seen in someone so young. It's really quite extraordinary."

"So you've formed an attachment?" Belgrave asked.

"Yes. I believe so. My intention is to speak with her father tonight, though I fear he might not approve."

"Why wouldn't he?" Edward asked. He knew the Earl of Oakland well and could not imagine him ever denying any of his children their happiness. "If you are the man Emily wants, he'll have no objections since you're obviously from a good family and..." The earl's dark expression gave him pause. "What is it?"

"Lord Oakland's father is dead because of my grandfather."

The words hung in the air, accentuated by the ensuing silence. Edward stared at Montsmouth. They all did. "Would you care to elaborate?" Edward eventually asked when nobody else said a word.

"You know Lord Oakland's father and Lord Duncaster were killed at sea?" When Edward nodded, Montsmouth said, "That's because my grandfather betrayed them." He went on to explain what had happened and how he'd initially come to Thorncliff in search of the exact same treasure the Huntleys sought.

"So the rumors are true?" Belgrave asked.

"They are," Edward confirmed. "I know from Fiona that several clues to it were uncovered when she and her family were here during the summer, though it has yet to be found."

"Perhaps now, with this extra bit of information from Montsmouth, doing so might be more possible," Lamont said. "If it consists of more than a jewelry box, then it must be hidden in a room large enough to accommodate it."

"The only problem is, no such room seems to exist," Montsmouth said. "Lady Emily says her brother Spencer took a look at the blueprints of Thorncliff when he was last here. They searched every room that was on it. And while secret tunnels and an underground villa have since been found, the treasure has not."

"Well, perhaps we should all try looking again," Belgrave said. "Fresh eyes might offer a different perspective."

"Lady Fiona and I have deduced that it must be on the ground floor." Edward took a moment to fill them in on the conversation she and he had had on the issue and the places they'd searched since then. "Lord Duncaster's study was a dead end, by the way."

"I propose we keep our minds open," Lamont said. "If all of these secret passages and rooms exist as you claim, there might be more. The trick will be finding them."

"You're right," Montsmouth said, "but even if we

do and the treasure is there, that still doesn't solve the problem of my heritage."

"Does Lady Emily know of it?" Edward asked.

Montsmouth nodded. "She does."

"And she is willing to accept it?"

"Yes."

"Then I'd advise you not to mention it to Oakland." Seeing the look of apprehension in Montsmouth's eyes, Edward added, "What happened was beyond your control. You had nothing to do with it personally. So why put a stumbling block in your path when there's no need for it?"

"I feel as though I ought to be honest."

"And you have been with Lady Emily, whom you plan to marry. You are not in debt, your title is unblemished, and there is no scandal attached to your name. Don't let your grandfather's poor judgment ruin your future."

Montsmouth nodded. "I'll think on it."

"In the meantime," Edward said, "we've yet to hear about you and Lady Rachel, Belgrave. Personally, I have to say I am thrilled to learn of your interest in her. Truth be told, her chance of ever marrying was looking rather dim, and lord knows she's been against it. If you have the power to make her happy, then I'm all for it."

"I must confess I admire her a great deal," Belgrave said. "She's wonderfully clever, with a touch of sarcastic wit I find rather appealing. Of course, she has yet to show an interest in receiving any amorous attention from me, but I do believe she might begin to do so soon. I think my interest in her work is what draws her at the moment."

"I've no doubt about it," Edward told him. "Lady

Rachel lives for her experiments, so meeting someone who wishes to know more about them must be compelling for her. Not to mention the fact she's probably in desperate need of kissing."

Belgrave blanched. "I beg your pardon?"

Edward grinned. "She has been wound up tight ever since she was little. No doubt she'll combust in your arms if you let her."

"Good God," Belgrave murmured.

"Precisely," Edward agreed. He drained his glass and set it on the table. "I find it to be an extraordinary coincidence that we should all find compatible partners during our stay here." He rose to his feet. "Shall we go in search of our quarries?"

Voicing their agreement, his friends stood and followed him from the room.

CHAPTER THIRTEEN

HAVING FINISHED THEIR TEA IN the parlor, Fiona and her sisters decided to go in search of everyone else. Lady Duncaster had gone to take Christmas baskets to the local tenants earlier, and their parents had gone with her.

"Don't you think they'll be back soon?" Laura asked while they headed toward the foyer. "I hoped to speak with them about something."

"About Lamont?" Fiona asked with a nudge to her sister's side. Rounding a corner, they saw the gentlemen coming toward them, and Fiona quietly added, "Speaking of which."

"Ladies," Chadwick said as he and his friends drew to a halt before them. His eyes darted toward Fiona, lingering on her long enough to cause a small tremor to race down her spine. Smiling, he gave his attention to her sisters. "The sun is out, so we thought we might take advantage. How does a ride to the village sound?"

"Like a marvelous idea," Fiona blurted with far more enthusiasm than she'd intended. Heating beneath everyone's attention, she deliberately tempered her tone and said, "It will be nice to get out for a bit, and since it is winter, one must do so when there's an opportunity."

The corner of Chadwick's mouth twitched with a hint of humor. "Quite right. I'll ask the butler to arrange for a couple of carriages to be brought round, if everyone is in agreement?"

"An outing sounds like a lovely idea," Emily said. Rachel and Laura concurred, and twenty minutes later, after collecting their pelisses, gloves, and bonnets, the ladies were escorted outside by the gentlemen.

Chadwick led Fiona toward the first carriage. His hand steadily clasping hers, he helped her up. "Will you ride with us, Lamont?" he called to the duke, while Fiona made herself comfortable on the forward facing bench. A second later, Laura climbed in, claiming the spot beside Fiona so Lamont and Chadwick could sit opposite.

"Ready?" Chadwick asked. He tapped the roof of the carriage once everyone gave their consent, and the conveyance took off.

Fiona glanced out the window at the passing scenery of naked trees and barren landscapes still covered in a thin layer of white. She dared not look at Chadwick for fear of what it might do to her and of what he might see in her gaze. The possibility of his discovering how drastically her feelings for him had changed was a horrifying notion indeed. She still hadn't come to terms with this sudden awareness that filled her whenever he was near and did not quite understand what it meant, much less what to do with it. He was a friend – a very close one.

If she gave but a hint of her heart's desire, he

would probably tell her how honored he was right before he tried to convince her that it was nothing more than a passing fancy. After all, he was a grown man with vast amounts of experience while she…she was little more than a silly girl capable of making him laugh. It would be humiliating to have him dismiss her as such. Worse than that, it would lead to an awkwardness between them that she vehemently wanted to avoid.

Over the past few days while he'd helped her search for the jewelry box, her attraction toward him had grown. She could feel herself savoring every glance and every touch they happened to share. Then he would say something silly or laugh, reminding her she was like a sister. It was all she ever would be, and if she were wise, she would stop hoping for more right now, before it was too late.

"That bonnet of yours is exceptionally pretty, Fiona," Chadwick said, his voice breaking through her secret ponderings and forcing her attention back to him.

She turned to face him, allowing a quick glance at Lamont whose steady gaze remained fixed on Laura with whom he conversed in a whisper. They were discussing the plot for the novel Laura was writing, and Fiona couldn't help but appreciate the attention and interest the duke was affording her sister.

Allowing her gaze to return to Chadwick's, she forced a smile and said, "Thank you. It was a gift from Mama for my birthday."

"I'm sorry I couldn't attend." His eyes held hers while his jaw seemed to clench, all joviality gone in favor of a far more serious expression. Unnerved by it, Fiona did her best to push back her rising discomfort. "I trust the novel I sent you was to your liking?"

"Indeed." He'd given her a copy of *Emma* which she'd happily devoured over the course of an evening. She'd read it three more times since. "I believe I sent you a letter of thanks. Did you not receive it?"

"Oh yes. Of course I did." He cleared his throat, averted his gaze for a second, and then allowed it to latch onto hers once more. His eyes appeared slightly darker now, and the effect was such that Fiona felt her heart tremble.

No.

No, no, no.

She had to get her silly nerves under control. "It was a good story," she managed to say.

"I thought so too."

His response surprised her. "You've read it?"

He finally smiled the sort of smile she was used to. It allowed her to relax a little as he told her gently, "I had to know what I was giving you, so yes, I bought my own copy."

"And?" They finally seemed to be returning to their usual sense of camaraderie. "What did you think of it?"

"Obviously, I liked it, or I wouldn't have given it to you."

"You might simply have thought it would appeal to me without actually liking it yourself."

Grinning, he dipped his head in acquiescence. "A possibility, to be sure, but far from the truth. If you must know, I enjoyed the author's depiction of class and the wit with which she writes."

"That is why I admire her work," Laura said, joining the conversation. "If I can only produce a novel on par with hers, I would be more than content."

"My lady," Lamont said, "I have every confidence you will succeed in that endeavor."

Laura blushed. Lowering her lashes, she shyly thanked him for the compliment.

"What I especially liked was the plot," Chadwick continued, this time looking at Laura.

"The idea of two longtime friends discovering they are in love with each other?" Laura asked. She glanced at Fiona, who immediately felt her cheeks flame with awareness.

"It was an interesting premise," Chadwick said, "though I wonder why it took them so long to recognize their feelings."

"Perhaps because there wouldn't have been a book if they'd figured it all out in the first chapter," Fiona pointed out, in an effort to dismiss the subject entirely. It was far too close to her own predicament for comfort, and the longer they lingered on it, the more likely it was that Chadwick might see straight through her.

His smile faltered. He knit his brow and quietly said, "You make an excellent point, Fiona." The carriage drew to a halt, and he glanced out the window. "Looks like we're here."

They alit in quick succession, reuniting with the rest of their party on the pavement. "Shall we visit the haberdashery first?" Emily asked. "I should like to buy some ribbon if I may."

"I'll escort you," Montsmouth said, quickly stepping up beside her and offering his arm.

Fiona watched her sister smile at the earl with stars in her eyes. He looked equally besotted, and Fiona couldn't quite stop the ache that started to form in her chest. Especially when he lowered his head to whisper something in Emily's ear. Emily laughed, and they started across the street with Laura and Lamont, Rachel and Belgrave following behind.

"Do you wish to join them?" Chadwick asked.

With little interest in any of the items the shop had to offer, Fiona shook her head. "I would rather stop by the cobbler, if there is one, so I can look for a new pair of walking boots. Furlined ones, if possible."

"I'll go with you." He called across to the others so they knew where he and Fiona were headed.

"I'd hate to keep you from your own interests," she said. Going alone in a village she wasn't familiar with was probably not the best of ideas, yet she felt a distinct need to add some distance between them.

"My only interest right now is in keeping you company, Fiona."

"Oh." They started along at a moderate pace. An unusual silence fell between them, and for the first time in her life, Fiona had no idea of what to say.

"The weather is pleasant," Chadwick finally murmured.

"Yes," she agreed.

Reaching the cobbler, Chadwick opened the door so she could enter. He followed her inside the moderately sized space, keeping close while she spoke to the clerk – a middle aged man who introduced himself as Mr. Smith.

"I believe I have precisely what you're looking for," Mr. Smith said. He asked them to wait a moment before disappearing into another room. Returning, he placed a lovely pair of light brown boots lined with rabbit fur on the counter. "These should keep your feet nice and warm."

"May I try them on?"

"Of course. Allow me to—"

"I'll help her ladyship if she requires assistance," Chadwick cut in.

"Of course," Mr. Smith agreed, politely handing the boots over to him. "I'll be in the back, so ring the bell if you need me."

Blinking, Fiona tried to comprehend what had just transpired. She gave her attention to Chadwick, who'd obviously taken complete control of her shoe shopping. "May I?" she asked, attempting to reach for the boots he was holding.

He drew them away from her, walked toward a chair, and crouched down beside it. "Come have a seat, will you?"

She stared at him. "What on earth are you doing?"

"Ensuring these boots fit you properly." Looking up at her, he produced a boyish grin that instantly turned her insides to mush.

She couldn't let him help her, she realized. It wouldn't be proper or even survivable, given the sparks that were presently jumping about in her belly at the idea of him doing so. "You will *not* be touching my feet, Chadwick. I am perfectly capable of trying those boots on my own."

"Stop protesting, will you?" He waved her closer, and she blew out a breath of pure exasperation. Reluctantly, she crossed the floor and took a seat.

"There. That wasn't so difficult. Was it?"

"No," she lied. She dropped a look at his upturned face and saw nothing but amicable friendship in the depths of his eyes. Pushing aside her jittery emotions with pure force of will, she held out her hand. "Now hand me the boots."

He laughed up at her with the same sort of playfulness that had always made her appreciate his company. "Do you plan on putting them on over your other pair?"

Before she could answer, he'd snatched up her right foot and placed it upon his bended knee. She instinctively squeaked. "What are you doing?"

"Helping you get these things off." He went to work on the laces.

His head was bowed to the task, so she could no longer see his expression, for which she was glad since it meant he could not see hers either. Heavens, she probably looked like a dumbfounded fool in danger of combusting at the prospect of what was to follow.

Her pulse leapt when the boot eased around her ankle, and then it was carefully pulled away and…oh dear God! She felt her heel resting against the palm of his hand, his thumb and ring-finger cradling her ankle, and her heart almost seized in response to the wave of desire that followed. Her breaths were shallow. All she could do was stare down at the top of his head, quite unable to utter a word while he crouched there, his hand shifting ever so slightly against her silk stocking. It was enough to send darts of pleasure shooting straight up her legs.

Drawing a sharp breath, she willed him to move.

Except he didn't. Why wasn't he moving?

She shook her foot. "Chadwick." She finally managed to get one word out of her dry mouth.

With a start, he reached for one of the new boots, slid it carefully into place, and did up the laces. "How does it fit?" Looking up, he met her gaze.

His brown eyes conveyed an element of warmth that told her he truly cared for her answer. Still, there was nothing to suggest he'd been any bit as affected by touching her foot as she had been. In fact, he didn't look bothered at all, which naturally bothered *her* all the more.

"Perfectly," she told him succinctly. She wiggled her toes back and forth inside the boot.

"Are you sure?"

"Yes. Why wouldn't I be?"

"Because you sound annoyed."

She expelled a breath and did her best to calm herself. It wasn't his fault she was turning into an imbecile in his presence. Only that it *was* his fault. Of course it was. Entirely. Curse him for looking so devilishly handsome and curse her for noticing.

"Forgive me," she said as she tugged her foot out of his hold and set it on the floor, "but I don't think you ought to help me with this any further."

"I've upset you."

He stood and turned his attention on a display shelf, though not fast enough for her to miss the distinct look of pain in his eyes. For reasons she couldn't understand, she'd hurt him. Which made no sense. Chadwick was not easily hurt by anyone. He always brushed words off with a laugh and a shrug of his shoulders. All she'd done was prevent him from doing something that would have been considered monumentally inappropriate if any other man, besides a relation, had offered to do it.

So perhaps that was it then? Perhaps he was able to feel her withdrawal from him, even though she'd tried her best to hide it. And since the last thing she wanted was to slight him in any way, she carefully told him, "No. I appreciate everything you do for me, Chadwick." He turned to face her with the sort of hopefulness that lifted her spirits. "Everything you've always done for me. You know this, surely."

"I do, and yet I cannot help but feel as though things have changed between us." He took a step forward, his intense brown eyes boring into the center of her soul. "Would you tell me if they have, Fiona?"

Swallowing, she did her best to remain as still as possible while her heart bounced about in her throat. "Nothing has changed, Chadwick." She managed to speak the words with an element of certainty that impressed even her. "I consider you a brother, and I always will. You must never doubt that."

His jaw flexed, and for a second she was certain she'd offended him yet again. But then he seemed to relax, and his fingers shot out to nudge her beneath her chin. A smile followed as he said, "I'm so glad to hear it, Fiona." Bending down, he quickly helped her replace the left boot she wore with the new one. "Now then, stand up and take a turn of the room, will you? We need to make sure they're a good fit before purchasing them."

She did what he suggested, all the while feeling as though she'd sacrificed part of herself and perhaps even part of him. The lie had been necessary though, because to confess the truth would have ruined everything she'd ever held dear. "They're good," she told him after a few paces back and forth.

He rang the bell for the clerk to return, and five minutes later they were back outside on the pavement, with a package containing her old boots tucked under Chadwick's arm and her growing love for him buried inside her miserable heart.

CHAPTER FOURTEEN

"DO YOU WANT TO CONTINUE searching for the jewelry box?" Edward asked Fiona when they returned to Thorncliff later.

He watched her hesitate for a moment – long enough to convey her reluctance and make his heart bleed – but then she smiled as if all was as it should be between them. "I would like that a great deal."

While common sense told him to leave her alone, he couldn't seem to stop himself from craving any small amount of time he might have left in her company. After all, Christmas would soon be over, and then they would part ways again – this time for much longer than ever before since he meant to add more distance between them. It was the only way for him to survive the truth she'd delivered with such painful accuracy, he'd felt his heart torn in two.

I consider you a brother, and I always will.

All hope had crumpled in an instant. And yet, while they were both still here, he would bask in her presence, absorbing each moment so it might be preserved to memory. This would be all he'd have left of her later, because staying near her and watching her marry another…that was not the sort of torture he planned to endure.

"Has Emily told you Montsmouth came here looking for the same thing as you?" he asked, once she'd handed over her packages to a footman and told her sisters she'd see them later.

They crossed the foyer and headed down a hallway, arriving in the Turkish salon shortly after. "Not the exact same thing," Fiona said. She started running her hands across the wall in search of any inconsistencies. "He looks for paintings and books. I look for a family heirloom."

Edward studied a painting that hung on the wall. It portrayed a scene from a harem with women lounging on mounds of cushions, veils shrouding their faces. "True. I was thinking it might be an idea for us all to work together – get your sisters and the other gentlemen involved. We'd cover more ground and… Hmm…Look at this."

"What is it?"

She came to stand beside him, and her shoulder grazed his arm as she looked at where he was pointing. A sharp pang of need shot straight through his limbs. Stilling, he did his best to suppress the urge to pull her into his arms and do what he'd wanted to do for so long – to kiss her senseless. In the shop earlier, holding her delicate foot in his hand, he'd been rendered both speechless and insensible, the urge to slide his hand higher and offer a more intimate caress so potent, all he'd been able to do was stay perfectly still lest he act on that urge.

Thankfully, he'd managed to restrain himself, and he would continue to do so now while she leaned in slightly, her citrusy scent assailing his senses and luring him closer until—

"Is that a peep hole?" she asked.

"Ahem…" He straightened himself and gave a stiff nod. "Yes. I believe so." It was tiny and extremely well hidden next to the frame. He never would have spotted it if he hadn't been searching.

"So then one of the secret passageways ought to be right behind here." Her voice held an edge of excitement that managed to ease Edward's tension. "Richard says he used them frequently when he was here. So did Chloe and her husband." She turned with bright enthusiasm. "Do you think we might explore it?"

"I don't see why not as long as we're able to find a way into it." He pressed his palm firmly against the wall. When it failed to give way, he slid his gaze toward the corner of the room where a beautifully carved cabinet stood. He walked toward it.

"You don't suppose there's a door behind there?" Fiona followed directly behind him, her excitement rolling off her in waves.

"It's as good a guess as any. Unless the entrance to the passageway is from somewhere else, but considering the peephole, I believe there must be some means of access from this room." He stood in front of the cabinet, studying it for a moment before applying a bit of pressure to the front of it. It remained where it was.

"Perhaps if you pull?"

He tried that next but it still didn't budge, so he opened the top door and searched the interior, reaching behind some candles that stood like soldiers in their holders and running his fingers across the wood in the back. When he touched a knob jutting out from the side, he stopped and took a deep breath.

"What is it?" Fiona asked. She moved nearer, trying to see.

It was more than he could bear. "Perhaps if you step back a bit, I'll be better able to figure that out," he said. His voice was as strained as he was, but it was the best he could do under the circumstances. As it was, he was balancing on a thin line that threatened to break at any second.

"Very well."

She sounded disgruntled, which almost made him laugh. If either of them had cause for such emotion, it was surely he. But he was intent on maintaining his composure, so he focused on moving the knob, fumbling slightly until the slippery piece of metal gave way, and he heard a distinct click. The cabinet moved – not much, but enough for him to know he'd met with success.

Pulling his arm back, he grabbed one of the candles, along with an available tinderbox. Then he closed the door to the cabinet and pulled the entire piece of furniture back from the wall to reveal a dark entrance.

"Oh my goodness," Fiona murmured, brushing right past him to peer inside. She glanced at him over her shoulder. "It smells a bit musty."

"I'm sure it does." Stepping up behind her, he gave the space some consideration. "It's probably full of spiders too, and we both know how much you hate those."

"Yes. I really do, but I'm determined to see this through, Chadwick." Her voice was firm and unyielding.

"Very well then." He opened the tinderbox, struck a piece of flint, and lit the candle. "Follow me, Fiona."

She did so without argument, closing the hidden doorway behind them until the candle remained their only source of light. The space was narrower than he'd expected, his shoulders almost brushing against either side of it as they made their way forward. Fiona's warmth radiated against his back in her effort to stay as close as possible without actually climbing onto him. A grim smile captured his lips. If he'd only refrained from mentioning the spiders, she might have kept her distance, and he might have managed to keep his sanity.

The thought had barely formed before he felt a bit of thin and sticky film clinging snugly to his forehead. He wiped it away with his free hand right before Fiona let out a squeal and grabbed hold of his arm. "Get it off, get it off, get it off!" She clutched at him, and he almost dropped the candle as he turned toward her, illuminating her terrified face and the spindly spider that crawled across her forehead, desperately thwarting her flapping hand.

"Hold still," he said, applying his most commanding tone in an effort to make her comply.

She immediately stopped moving, her eyes squeezed tightly together while her rapid breaths conveyed her anxiety and she waited for him to save her. Reaching out, he snatched the arachnid between his fingers and tossed it aside. "There. It's gone." He prepared to turn back around and continue walking when she suddenly launched herself forward, straight into his arms.

Holy hell!

"Thank you," she murmured against his shoulder, her face pressed firmly into his brushed wool jacket. Her hands gripped at his shoulders as though he offered some safe escape from her frightening surroundings.

"Perhaps we ought to go back. The Turkish salon isn't far."

"No." She shook her head against him, and he could feel heat penetrating every layer of clothing he wore when she expelled each breath.

Rigidly, he lowered his free arm, allowing the limb to fall loosely around her waist. "It was only a spider, Fiona. Nothing more."

"I know, Edward. I…I just hate them so much."

He couldn't form a response. Not when she'd used his given name for the second time in her life. And the way she'd said it – as if he and he alone offered every bit of security she'd require—made his chest tighten until a ragged breath was squeezed from his lungs.

Unable to stop himself, he allowed his palm to rest against the small of her back, to revel in the feel of her luscious body pressed up against his. Oh, he would likely rot in hell for taking advantage of her innocent need for reassurance like this. But to not do so would lead to regret later. So he held her close until he felt her relax.

"Fiona?"

"Hmm?"

The way she murmured and pressed slightly closer made him wonder if… Perhaps… He shook his head. No. There was no point in dreaming when she'd given him no reason to hope. Quite the contrary. So he lowered his arm and asked her seriously, "Shall we continue?"

She let go of him faster than someone might drop a piece of hot coal. "Of course we should."

He wasn't sure whether to be offended by her sudden dismissal or not. Hesitating only a moment, he chose not to dwell on it, asking her simply, "Are you going to be all right in here?"

"I will be fine, Chadwick. Please light the way."

Ah, so they were back to the honorific.

He already missed the closeness they'd shared moments earlier, however brief or one-sided it had been. But since he wasn't willing to wallow in self-pity, he turned away and continued walking while floorboards creaked beneath his feet. Holding his hand out in front of his face, he brushed aside upcoming cobwebs and received no further complaints from Fiona, for which he was glad.

"There's a corner here," he said when they reached a sharp turn. "Watch your step." Rounding it, Edward held up the candle to illuminate the space ahead of them. "It looks like this might go on for a while."

"How can that be? Thorncliff has windows, and all of the rooms have doors. The passageways have to be broken up somehow, either by stairs or…or something else."

"You're right." He started forward once more, then stopped and dropped to a crouch.

"What are you doing?"

Lowering the candle, he illuminated the space between the floor and the wall. "There's a slight decline. If I'm not mistaken, we've been walking downward all of this time, in which case we might soon be beneath Thorncliff altogether."

"Perhaps this leads to the villa, then, or connects to the other underground tunnels we know about?"

"It's a possibility." He stood and continued walking. "It is also possible we're headed in an entirely different direction, though I could be wrong."

"But if you're right?"

"After entering the passage, we walked parallel with the east wall of the Turkish salon, heading north. Did you count our paces?"

"No. Did you?"

He nodded. "We took thirty, which would have placed us well past the salon, perhaps somewhere beneath the hallway that leads toward the grand staircase."

"And then we made a turn," Fiona said.

"Yes. Straight west." Resuming his pace, he spoke while he walked. "The underground villa and the tunnels that lead to the sea are in the opposite direction. Right now, I'd say we're heading toward the foyer."

"Uncharted territory?" She couldn't have sounded more thrilled.

He smiled in response. "Quite so, my little adventuress."

She didn't respond with the quick retort he'd expected. Instead, she kept quiet for several seconds before quietly saying, "You do realize I'm no longer a child, Chadwick?"

"I…er… It's sometimes difficult to remember," he teased in an effort to hide how aware he'd become of her womanly charms.

"You're impossible," she muttered.

But he didn't miss the hint of annoyance in her voice as she said it, so he came to a halt and turned to face her, expelling a deep breath. "I'm sorry, Fiona. I didn't mean to upset you. Obviously you've…" He struggled against the dryness in his mouth while he stared down into her dimly lit eyes. "You're quite grown up now, I see, but I do hope that won't affect our friendship in any way."

"No." She averted her gaze, hiding whatever expression might lurk there.

He forced himself to continue – to say what was necessary. "I've always enjoyed our repartees, your wit, and your smart rejoinders. This," he waved a hand to indicate their surroundings, "is one of the things I love about you."

Her eyes had snapped back to his. "One of the things you love about me?"

Jesus Christ and all his apostles!

Her astonishment was undeniable. She stared up at him with wide eyes that made him want to kick himself for revealing so much. "Of course," he said, forcing a nonchalant tone. "You're like family."

She nodded. "We've had some fun times together over the years," she said, and he breathed a sigh of relief at her change in subject. "Do you remember when we climbed onto the stable roof at Oakland House a couple of years ago?"

Grinning at the memory, he swung away from her and recommenced walking. "When *you* climbed onto the stable roof, you mean? The only reason *I* went up was because you got stuck and needed someone to save you."

"I still can't believe you didn't tell Spencer about

it. Or anyone else for that matter."

"And get you into trouble? I couldn't allow that after you'd covered for me with your cook."

"She was furious when she discovered the missing supplies in the pantry."

"As I recall, she needed those things for supper, though I didn't realize it at the time."

Fiona laughed. "We had broth that day while you—"

"Enjoyed a lovely picnic with Lady Jemima." *Damn!* He bit his tongue, but the name was already out.

"So that's who you snuck off to see. Will you tell me what happened with her?"

"Nothing." He didn't plan to elaborate.

"Please?" When he said nothing further, she quietly asked, "Did she break your heart?"

No. Only you are capable of doing so.

He winced, hating the disgruntled mood he was suddenly in. "She was a sweet girl, but she and I weren't meant to be."

"But you courted her? With the picnic and all?"

"I was never alone with her if that's what you think. She brought friends, and we had a pleasant enough afternoon. The next time I saw her, she was getting engaged to Baron Whitham."

"Oh."

That was all she said, and for reasons he couldn't explain, that single syllable grated unlike anything else in the world. "She doesn't matter," he found himself saying.

"Of course not," she murmured in a way that suggested she did not believe him.

Deciding to drop the subject since only one thing

might convince her Lady Jemima held no sway over his feelings, he gave his attention to the place ahead where the passageway split in a T. "These are some pretty big stones." He passed the light over the wall in the next passageway. "There's been nothing but wood until now, but even the ground is different here. There are stone slabs instead of planking, so I'm guessing we've reached the cellar level."

"So then the foyer ought to be directly overhead?"

"I think so." He held the candle out in front of him. "This tunnel leads off in both directions."

"Do you want to continue exploring?"

He considered the hopefulness with which she spoke. "One hundred paces in that direction," he said, pointing toward the right. "If we don't find another entry to Thorncliff by then, I think we ought to return the way we came. We can always come back later with the others and some proper lanterns."

"Agreed."

He began counting off his steps. *One, two, three, four, five…*

"What made you decide to go this way?" Fiona asked.

"If I'm right and we're underneath the foyer walking south, then going the opposite way would have led us out of Thorncliff to only God knows where." *Six, seven, eight…*

"How clever of you."

Edward drew to a halt. "I'm good for more than a laugh, Fiona."

"I…I'm sorry. I didn't mean it like that." Her

hand touched his arm, and he inwardly groaned at the pleasure of having her so near. "I think the world of you, Chadwick. You must know that?"

"Of course I do." It was just the pain of knowing she'd never be his that made him lash out. "But I'm also aware of what people say and of what they think." He blew out a breath and then leaned against the wall. "It's my own fault, I suppose, for always making fun in public – for always being ready with a joke and trying to make people laugh. Few people take me seriously."

"I do," she said, her hand squeezing against his arm while she spoke. "There's no denying I've always been drawn to your mischievous nature and this propensity you have for silliness. Being around you is amusing, Chadwick, and the fact you gave your attention to me as a child when others your age ignored me is something I'll always appreciate."

He grunted slightly on impulse. "You were quite precocious."

"The point is," she continued without addressing his comment, "you're so much more than what people think. Your success in business – the investments you've made in cotton mills, shipping, and the Mayfair Chronicle to name a few— is most impressive, not to mention the kindness with which you treat your tenants."

Speechless, he stared at her upturned face, while candlelight flickered across her brow and cheekbones. There was some sort of desperation in her eyes – a keenness to make him see himself as she did. The honesty of it practically slayed him.

"How do you know all of this?" He'd never spoken of his responsibilities before or of how he made his money.

Shrugging, she drew back and let his arm go. "Spencer mentioned it once. I was interested, so I kept pestering him about it until he eventually escaped to his bedchamber and closed the door in my face."

"You were interested?" It was all his mind could comprehend at the moment.

"Well, yes. Knowing how money is made is a useful bit of information to have, I should think. Even if men have a tendency to keep such things from women. So once I'd gotten Spencer talking, I did what I could to gain as much knowledge as possible."

Of course, that had to be it. Because to think she might have had a more personal interest in him was obviously ludicrous. Still, he needed to take something with him – something more than the friendship she offered. So he reached up and placed the palm of his hand against her cheek, enjoying her startled expression and the warmth of her skin beneath his touch. It was so soft, he imagined stroking his fingers across it forever. Breathing was no longer as simple as it had been seconds before.

If only…

He retracted his hand before she might see how he felt. *Dear God, please don't let her see*. "We should probably keep moving," he heard himself say in a voice both distant and foreign. She didn't reply, and he could practically hear the walls rising between them as he acknowledged the love he felt and that she'd never feel the same way. "Here. There's an alcove." He pushed the candle inside and looked around. "Stairs. Come along."

They started up the uneven stone steps that sagged in the middle. "Are you all right?" He wanted to hear her voice.

"It's a bit steep but I'm managing."

"Good." No other words were spoken until they reached the top. Here, the floor was once again made of wooden planks. Edward moved along, Fiona close behind, until he spotted a crack in the wall running all the way to the ceiling. He pressed his hand carefully against it until it gave way with a creak. "It's the green salon," he said, and stepped out into the room where several curious faces were watching their unusual arrival.

"I say," Montsmouth remarked from his spot in an armchair. "Would it not have been simpler to come through the door?"

"I didn't realize there was a tunnel right there," Emily added. "Fiona, you look a fright, all covered in dust and heavens knows what else. If I might offer a suggestion, you'd best go change."

"I plan on doing so right away," Fiona said while Edward closed the wall paneling behind them.

"You too, Chadwick," Lady Duncaster said. "Come back when the cobwebs have been removed from your hair. You can tell us all about your little adventure, while enjoying a cup of mulled wine."

"Thank you, your ladyship." Edward saw Fiona was already exiting the room.

He started to follow, but was stopped by Lord Oakland's broad figure as he stepped into his path. Dipping his head, the earl whispered in Edward's ear, "We've always considered you family, Chadwick, but I think it's important to remember that you're not – not really. Going off on your own with

Fiona might not be your best course of action. I hope there's no cause for concern?"

The warning could not have been clearer. "Of course not, my lord. It won't happen again." With this assurance, Edward left the room at a brisk pace and with the distinct feeling he'd landed in his own private hell.

CHAPTER FIFTEEN

SEATED AT THE HEAD OF the table, Emilia, the Dowager Countess of Duncaster, glanced over the rim of her wine glass and studied each of her guests in turn. She'd been right to gather them all here for the holidays, though doing so had had nothing to do with loneliness, as she'd stated in the invitations she'd sent them. Sipping her claret, she considered the newly formed couples and smiled. Everything was moving along precisely according to plan, though she couldn't help but wonder if anyone else was aware of the fact.

Amused, she set her glass down and dipped her spoon into the pudding Cook had prepared for desert. She'd always had a fondness for sweets, and her late husband, George, God bless him, had happily indulged her. She swallowed the painful reminder of her loss with a bit of custard, savoring the thick and creamy flavor of vanilla as it swirled around her mouth. *Delicious.*

"Lady Duncaster. Will you partner with me for a game of whist later?" Lady Oakland asked.

Setting her spoon down, Emilia answered the request with a smile. "Sounds delightful." She considered those present. "Who are we playing against?"

"Rachel and Belgrave," came the reply.

"Ho!" Leaning forward, Emilia speared the viscount with her eyes. "She's a devil with numbers, that one." She jutted her chin toward Rachel. "It's a skill that favors her in card play, so I trust you'll be able to keep up?"

"She and I have every intention of obliterating the two of you." Belgrave spoke with a kind voice that only accentuated his challenge.

Emilia laughed. "I'm sure you do." Picking her glass back up, she saluted him with a wink that made him chuckle. Oh yes, he'd do well with Rachel, Emilia decided. No doubt about that.

But there was more to discuss than their entertainment for the evening. "I've decided to host a ball this coming Saturday. Invitations will go out tomorrow to all the gentry within a two-hour ride."

"That's wonderful news," Laura said, already smiling with expectation.

"We'll have to go to town," Emily told her mother with a pointed look in Rachel's direction.

Rachel froze. "There's really no—"

"Of course we shall, dear," Marie, the Countess of Oakland, replied before her daughter could finish her protest. "We'll go tomorrow right after breakfast."

"Don't you fear the roads will be difficult for people to travel?" Lord Oakland asked Emilia. "Hosting a ball this time of year doesn't come without risk."

"Are you worried no one will come?" she asked.

Of course, she shared the concern, but if that were indeed to happen, there would still be the eleven of them as initially planned. No harm done.

"Not at all," Lord Oakland told her. "What I worry about is your having to put up everyone who chooses to attend on account of the fact they might not be able to return home again."

Very well. She hadn't considered that. But she did so now, her eyes squinting at the painting that hung on the far wall while she pondered her options. Eventually, she said, "There is room enough for all if that were to happen. And think of the fun we shall have then!"

"I doubt the footmen who will have to chop firewood will agree with you on that point," Lamont murmured.

"They might grumble a little at first, but I do make sure to pay them well, and I'll simply have to add a few more pounds, if need be, to sweeten the deal." Waving her hand, she dismissed all concern while saying jovially, "But why worry about the worst outcome before the need to do so arises? For all we know, we might have cloudless skies that evening."

Agreeing with her point, her guests finished off their meal and their wine before filing out of the dining room and heading toward the library, where gaming tables had been set up. It had been agreed that the men would enjoy their after-dinner drinks while playing, in order for them to save time. Emilia ensured each received either brandy or port, depending on their preference, and that cheroots and cigars were made readily available as well.

"I'll have one myself," she said, when the cheroots were passed around. She'd never taken issue with smoking in public, even though some sticklers did frown upon it. They could all go hang as far as she was concerned – stuck-up mood killers that they were.

"Shall I deal?" Belgrave asked.

"Go ahead," Marie told him. She'd always been a gentle lady with the sort of innate elegance many women would give a fortune to acquire. Emilia liked her a great deal although their personalities were vastly different and their ages at least two decades apart. And as far as her children were concerned…Well, Emilia had always thought of herself as their great-aunt, and with no children of her own to care for, she'd enjoyed watching them grow.

"You ought to try the sherry, Rachel," she said as she gathered her cards up into her hand and proceeded to put them in order.

"Thank you, but I think I'd prefer a tea."

Emilia chuckled. "Of course you would." Emilia waited for Belgrave to play before adding her king of spades to the mix. Rachel took the trick with the ace. "I do believe I'm going to challenge your inner scientist, Rachel." Emilia waved for a footman to approach the table. "Lady Rachel would like tea, please." The footman disappeared, and the next card was put into play.

"What do you mean about challenging me?" Rachel asked.

"Simply that I would like you to sample my entire collection of liquor while you are still here. As an experiment."

Belgrave raised an eyebrow but said nothing. Marie did not follow suit. "Are you trying to get my daughter foxed?" She pinned Emilia with her dazzling green eyes while responding to a three of hearts with a nine.

"Of course not." Pressing her lips together, Emilia allowed a few more cards to be played before saying, "I only want her to have a bit of fun, that is all."

"And you believe imbibing will be the answer?" Belgrave asked. "You assume Lady Rachel shares your opinion on what it means to enjoy life – that she feels unfulfilled in some way." He played the next card, the three of clubs. "But she is not you, my lady. She is her own person, and from where I'm sitting, that is a rather wonderful thing."

It took some effort for Emilia not to beam in response to Belgrave's declaration. "What a marvelous observation," she managed to say with a bland expression.

"He meant no offense," Rachel hastily added, this time leaping to his defense.

It was getting increasingly difficult for Emilia not to smile. Instead, she focused her attention on the last remaining cards in her hand and quietly muttered, "I think you're mistaken, my dear, but since I've always admired a man with a backbone, I can hardly say I mind. Belgrave was right to put me in my place."

"My lady," Belgrave began.

She shot him a chastising look. "Don't you dare ruin it with an apology."

He sat back in his seat.

Marie chuckled. "It looks as though you still have it in you, Emilia."

"What is that?"

"The ability to make a man squirm."

"Nonsense." Emilia played her last card, claiming the final trick. "Belgrave isn't squirming. He's counting his victory. Isn't that right, my lord?"

Dipping his head, he allowed a broad smile. "To win against the formidable Lady Duncaster is indeed an accomplishment to be savored."

She couldn't help but laugh in response. Neither could Rachel or Marie. The tea arrived, and they played a few more hands before Emilia felt she was ready to retire for the evening. "I hope you'll forgive me, but age demands I get some rest."

"I'll escort you up," Marie said, excusing herself to the rest of the room. "Will you be up soon, Phillip?" she asked her husband, who was still in the middle of a game with Lamont, Emily, and Laura. Montsmouth, who'd pulled up a chair, was looking over Emily's shoulder and offering occasional suggestions. Fiona and Chadwick, on the other hand, were nowhere in sight. They must have quit the room while she'd been distracted by the game.

"What do you think?" Marie asked as soon as the two of them were alone in the hallway.

Linking her arm with her friend's, Emilia gave her honest opinion. "I believe there's a good chance of success – more so than I would initially have imagined."

"I had my greatest doubts about Emily and Montsmouth. It still astounds me how right you were on that score."

"Let us hope so, Marie. Still, I would caution you not to get too excited. Nothing has been settled yet and…" She blew out her breath. "What on earth was your husband thinking when he chastised Chadwick?"

"You heard that, did you?"

"Considering the length of my ears, it was difficult for me not to since I was sitting the closest."

They reached the end of the hallway and started in the direction of the grand staircase. "I think he was hoping to make Chadwick aware of his feelings, though I fear he might have managed to scare him off instead."

"Frankly, I'm a bit disappointed in him and Fiona. Of all the matches we're hoping to make, I was certain the two of them would be the first." If only they'd be more aware of the other's regard.

"They have to risk their friendship, Emilia. That's no small thing."

"Yes. I am aware." She glanced at her friend. "It makes me want to interfere – shake some sense into them."

"I know," Marie said, "but when we decided on this course, we agreed all we would do was bring them together and give them the necessary opportunity for their affections to flourish. It has to come naturally or not at all."

Emilia knew she was right. Any further manipulation on their part would be a mistake. "At least they're looking for the treasure again. It's good for them to have something to work on together, but with only one week left, I worry it won't be enough."

"There's still the ball. I must say, that was a smart move on your part – an excuse for them to dance together and for him to see her at her best."

Emilia nodded. "That was my intention, although

I have to admit, the ball is mostly for Rachel's benefit." They reached the stairs and started their ascent at a moderate pace. "She needs a reason to dress up, not for Belgrave's sake alone, but for hers as well. I want her to feel the thrill of being admired."

"She certainly deserves to be." Marie shook her head. "I cannot believe I was so unaware of her scientific accomplishments."

"And Belgrave appreciates her worth. You can see it in his eyes whenever he looks at her, so I doubt it will be long now before he makes his intentions known to her."

"Perhaps at the ball?"

"That is what I am hoping for." They arrived at the top of the landing and began making their way down the hallway. "What about Montsmouth and Emily?"

Marie smiled. "He spoke to Philip earlier this evening. As did Lamont."

"Indeed?" This was excellent news. "So two of the gentlemen have made their intentions known. I trust they were given permission to court Emily and Laura?"

"Of course." Marie paused before saying, "As you know, we were a bit hesitant about Montsmouth. He's always seemed a bit odd to us, but Emily says she has her heart set on him. To be honest, we couldn't be happier for her or for Laura."

They reached Marie's bedchamber and stopped in front of the door. "If all goes according to plan," Emilia said, "you'll have all of your seven children settled in the space of a year. That's quite an achievement, my dear. Some might say sensational."

Marie smiled. "All I want is for them to be happy."

They said good night and parted ways, with Emilia continuing toward her own apartment at the far end of the wing. She'd found love a lifetime ago, and she had cherished every moment of it for as long as it had lasted. Now, she would take pleasure in ensuring others were able to enjoy what she'd once had – to feel the excitement born from a lover's kiss and the hope that bloomed with the knowledge of shared desires.

CHAPTER SIXTEEN

I T HAD BEEN EXACTLY TWENTY-SIX hours since Lady Duncaster had made her remark about the brandy. Standing in the empty parlor, Rachel observed the time. Midnight. She expelled a breath and approached the side table. The lantern she'd brought illuminated the room to satisfaction – enough for her to see what was in each bottle and crystal decanter. The various shades of amber liquid winked at her through the shadows. This had to be the silliest idea to have ever swamped her mind. But ever since she'd been challenged on a scientific basis, it had been impossible for her to ignore the possibility for an experiment.

The test was simple, really. She would have a sip from each bottle and write down her opinions in the notebook she'd brought along. Included therein would be flavors, sweetness, acidity, and so forth. Perhaps she'd even find something that stood out and be able to tell Lady Duncaster how well a particular spirit agreed with her. A smile filled her lips at that idea. She picked up the first bottle and poured a small measure into a glass. She took a sip, wincing in response to the strong flavor but forcing herself to swirl it around her mouth.

Hmm…

Not one of the best she'd ever had, but perhaps it wasn't too awful either. It was certainly spicy. She detected a subtle hint of fruit and caramel. Setting the glass aside, she jotted that down beside the name of the brandy she'd selected, a Courvoisier & Curlier from 1789. Next, was a Hennessy Cognac. She picked a clean glass and tasted this as well.

Oh!

It was bolder, perhaps even a bit warmer and with…what was that? The flavor eluded her even as it surprised her with its uniqueness. To her consternation, she had to admit it might be the best she'd ever tried. So she took another sip before moving on to the next. Five more bottles followed and then three carafes, two of which contained different brands of sherry. She liked the sweet one the best because it rolled down her throat like honey. *Mmmm.* Perhaps one more sip of that one as well…

"Lady Rachel?"

She clasped the carafe and spun toward the voice that had spoken. "Belgrave?" He stood a short distance away, which meant she had not heard him enter the room. "What on earth are you doing here?" Blinking, she tried to clear her head. It was starting to feel slightly fuzzy.

"I couldn't sleep and thought I'd get a drink, but I see you've beaten me to it."

"Hmm? Oh! You mean this?" She lifted the carafe she was holding. He raised his eyebrows and gave her a curious look that made her feel oddly warm all over. "This is just an experiment."

"In how to get foxed?"

"I am not…" She pushed out a breath and returned the carafe to its spot on the sideboard. "I know I had a brandy with you in the library, but that was mostly to see how you might react. I don't really make a habit of drinking on a regularly basis."

"Unless Lady Duncaster decides to goad you."

"She means well, you know, and she was right to push me a little. Besides, I find the flavors interesting. I never considered how different they could be. It's all tasted the same to me until now, when I'm actually focusing on the flavors."

He shrugged, then stepped forward and picked up a glass. He poured a measure of the Hennessy and raised it to his lips, drinking while his gaze lingered on her. "Did you try this one?" he asked, holding the glass toward her.

"I…I…Yes." She stared at the glass and at the large hand holding it. "It was probably my favorite, besides the sherry in that carafe over there. It was very good as well."

"Feel free to have a bit more if you like." He nudged the glass forward a tiny bit more.

Her mouth went dry. "But you've just drunk from there," she blurted without even thinking.

The edge of his mouth lifted. "I'm not diseased, if that's your concern."

"No. Of course you're not." Heavens, her heart was beating so fast she feared it might suddenly fly from her chest. "I merely think it might be rather inappropriate."

"Perhaps you're right." He remained where he was, completely still, his eyes searching hers until she fairly trembled beneath his gaze. Then, without warning, he turned away and strode across to the wall where Fiona and Chadwick had entered earlier. He set his palm against it and quietly asked, "Can you imagine finding the treasure while we're here?"

"Doing so does become more likely as we eliminate places during our search. I think Fiona's assessment of where to look is logical."

"You mean the ground floor area surrounding the foyer?"

She gave a concrete nod. "The other parts of the house have already been explored without success, and according to everyone else's accounts, not even the secret passageways have offered any clues."

"They also haven't been fully investigated." He raised his glass to his lips and sipped his brandy.

Their eyes met, and she felt her chest tighten. Lord, he was handsome. And when he looked at her like that, as though he held some decadent secret in the confines of his mind, she could practically feel herself melt in response. Jamming her knees together, she set her mind on remaining upright. She was not some silly female prone to swooning or any other ailments a weaker-minded individual might suffer when in the presence of such powerful masculinity.

"True."

The word did not carry the sort of conciseness she would have liked. Instead, it came out a whisper. Belgrave smiled as though hearing her every thought. *Annoying man.* Breaking eye contact, she snatched up one of the glasses she'd used earlier and poured herself some more Hennessy. It instantly calmed her nerves the moment she drank, and she finally understood the pleasure in such indulgence.

"Perhaps we could continue to search for it together?"

The question interrupted the momentary escape from reality the drink had offered. It reminded Rachel she wasn't alone. She turned toward Belgrave. Casually reclining against the backrest of the chair he now occupied, he kept his gaze firmly on her while he cradled his glass between his hands. His entire demeanor prompted a question that demanded an answer. "What is it you want from me, my lord?" He'd mentioned marriage one evening at dinner, but surely that had been a joke.

His eyes narrowed a fraction, and Rachel could not dismiss the change in his expression. It was almost as though he was caught between pain and pleasure. "Everything," he murmured.

She stilled. Surely she must have misheard him. "I beg your pardon?"

He flinched, appeared to collect himself as he straightened his posture, and cleared his throat. "Companionship, for starters." Looking unsatisfied with his comment, he set his glass aside and stood. "Might I ask you a personal question, my lady?"

"That depends," she hedged. He was coming toward her now, and she suddenly felt inclined to both flee and fling herself in his direction. How utterly absurd!

"What I wish to know," he said, stopping before her, "is what you truly desire from life." He leaned into her ever so slightly, crowding her with his much larger size and making her feel more vulnerable than ever before.

She drew a breath. "I..." What did she desire,

besides the obvious? She chose to lead with that. "To make a scientific discovery and to be acknowledged for it, in spite of my sex."

"As long as your determination does not waver, I see no reason why you cannot accomplish such a feat. But that was not what I was referring to."

"No?" She could barely breathe, he was so close.

"I'm aware of your academic dreams. You mentioned them the first night at supper, and we have spoken of them at great length since."

"So then?" What else could there possibly be?

He tilted his head, enough to allow the light to shift across the side of his face. "What about a husband, children, a family of your own? Do you plan to make room for that, or will you insist on living alone?"

"I never insist on anything, my lord." Why did she sound so breathless?

"Perhaps you should." His hand rose, and he was suddenly touching her shoulder. Small sparks of heat began to dance across her skin. "Perhaps," he continued, settling his hand more firmly against her, "you ought to let yourself want a whole lot more than the Royal Society's acceptance."

"I've done the calculations," she muttered. "To find a suitable match close at hand would be—"

"Impossible?"

Feeling weak, she only managed a nod.

"Then perhaps you should dare to dream of the impossible." His other hand swept aside a curl that had come undone from her coiffure and fallen across her face. "Unless, of course, you are immune to my affection, in which case I ask you to tell me so swiftly, so I may be released from my torment."

Understanding shot straight through her, piercing her with its sharp acuteness. "You…" She could write an endless amount of complicated equations, but right here, right now, she simply could not find the right words.

"I admire you, Lady Rachel." His thumb found her cheek, and the lightness of the pressure there was so incredibly soothing. "If you must know, you've managed to turn my whole world upside down."

"According to Newton," she stammered, finding her tongue, "the—"

"Let me say my piece." His dark eyes met hers with entreaty, and then he quietly added one simple word, "Please."

All she could do was stare back at him. It was as if he'd woven a spell. One from which there would be no escape. Her mind had certainly ceased to function at its full capacity. And her body…it was feeling things…little sensations that had started to form the moment he'd looked at her from across the table the very first evening at dinner. They'd been escalating ever since. Most notably when he was near.

A frown formed upon his forehead as if he was trying to think of what to say next. Eventually, he simply asked, "Would it surprise you if I were to say you are…" He paused then, just for a second, before hesitantly saying, "the most impressive woman I have ever had the pleasure of knowing?"

She shook her head, dumbfounded.

"I cannot imagine how you might feel about me. All I can do is hope that perhaps, in some small way, you might be willing to re-examine your position on marriage, that perhaps you'll consider the possibility that your statistical calculations have been wrong and that the perfect man for you is standing before you at this exact moment."

Feeling as though he was balancing on the tip of a pin, Arthur held his breath and watched while a series of complex emotions played across Lady Rachel's face. He'd never made such a declaration before, though he'd come close once where Lady Mary – now Mrs. Heartly – was concerned. But even then, while he'd held her in the highest regard and still did, their acquaintance had lacked the spark he now felt. Had they wed, it would have been an amicable marriage of convenience, but it would not have had the sort of substance Lady Rachel promised to provide.

It both surprised and pleased him to find he was equally attracted to her physical attributes and her mind. In fact, the mixture – her staid discipline coupled with an intellectual demand for knowledge – was more compelling than he ever would have imagined possible. The idea of possibly challenging her control and of broadening her horizons in a more physical capacity was so unbelievably enticing, he could scarcely stop himself from demanding a kiss.

Christ!

This woman had found some inexplicable means by which to challenge his gentlemanly ways. She tempted him to act without thought for propriety when he'd built his entire reputation on being respectable and decent. Now, his contemplations were bringing to life an inner rogue he'd never believed existed, while his actions… He curled his fingers into fists and allowed his nails to dig against his palms in an effort to force some restraint on himself. Lady Rachel bit her bottom lip as if in contemplation. She'd dropped her gaze to somewhere in the middle of his chest, prompting the curls she'd fashioned in recent days to fall slightly forward.

Arthur counted ten full seconds before she raised her chin to look back at him with resolve. "Is this how you honestly feel?"

"It is."

She swallowed, and he watched in fascination as her throat moved against the effort. "But I am plain and unexciting, my lord, while you are so…so…" A blush crept over her cheeks, and she averted her gaze.

"So what?" He couldn't help but ask.

Slowly, as though it took her tremendous effort, she allowed her gaze to slide back to his. "Handsome," she muttered, so low he could scarcely hear her. "Surely you'd want a prettier wife. After all, you are an earl – wealthy, by all accounts, and highly respected – so you could easily have your pick of available brides."

"The only woman I want is you." He took a small step closer and was pleased when she didn't back away, though she did suck in an audible breath. "You are beautiful, both inside and out, and if you ever suggest otherwise again, I might have to set you across my knees and spank some sense into you."

"Re-really?"

"Oh yes." He took another step, and the rogue within him sprang forward in full force, no doubt on account of her breathy voice. "So, my lady, what will it be? The possibility of sharing your future with me, or a life dedicated only to science? And before you answer, I can assure you I will support you in your scientific pursuits, but I wish to do so as your partner. I want to discuss your theories with you over tea and scones. I want to help you succeed, perhaps even invest in the lamp you plan on inventing."

"That does sound rather wonderful."

"Yes." Reaching up, he grabbed one of her curls and allowed it to slide between his fingers. "But there must also be time for you and me to indulge in other pursuits."

Her eyes had gone as wide as saucers. "Like what?"

"Well, for starters, I think kissing ought to be a crucial part of your education." He allowed his fingers to trail across her jawline in a feather-soft caress. Deliberately, he dropped his tone to a husky whisper before daring to ask, "What are your thoughts on the matter?"

She actually gulped, in the adorable sort of way that only an unschooled woman faced with the prospect of venturing down a forbidden path would do. And then she nodded. "I think kissing might be rather nice."

"Oh, it will be more than that," he promised as he finally pulled her close and wrapped his arms around her. "I dare say it's going to be delicious."

A hiss of breath escaped her in answer to that salacious comment. Her chin tipped up, and her eyes closed with an expectation that swiftly brought his lips to hers. The caress was sweet and gentle, the slowness of it complemented by the softest touch of pressure—a tempting elixir that threatened to be his undoing. It was so at odds with the fiery yearning roaring inside him – a dangerous need threatening to conquer her innocence.

Worse was the quivering murmur tumbling over her lips when he tightened his hold, the feel of her arms winding their way around his neck as she pressed herself into his body. Dear God, he could feel every part of her meld against him, and Christ, nothing in the world would ever compensate for such a glorious feeling.

"More," he murmured against her mouth before playfully drawing her lip between his teeth. The effect made her gasp, and he quickly took advantage, deepening the kiss with a skill that had taken years for him to master. He now applied every lesson he'd learned to coaxing a passionate response from Rachel, the need to make her reveal the wanton inside her so strong, it would not be denied.

Thankfully, she did not push him away as he might have feared. Instead, she followed his lead, exploring his mouth with such enthusiasm, he was hard pressed not to toss her onto the nearest sofa and have his wicked way with her right there in the parlor. Restraint was both his friend and his foe in that regard, but regret was going to be a devilish beast to deal with later, so he did what he could to hold back and to simply enjoy the flavor of brandy upon her tongue.

"That was…extraordinary," she said, when he finally found the will to let her withdraw. Raising her hand, she pressed her fingertips to her lips as if in wonder, then met his gaze with curious eyes. "Did I do all right?"

Her question practically slayed him. "My dearest, Rachel." Leaning forward, he brushed a kiss against her forehead. "You were wonderful."

"I'm sure I still have much to learn." Her cheeks burned bright in the dimly lit room, but she stayed where she was, valiantly staring back at him as though he held the key to her continued happiness.

"Of course you do, and I would be more than honored to teach you, if you're inclined to accept my suit."

She smiled then. "From a scientific point of view, I do believe there may be some benefit to doing so."

"Cheeky minx."

"From an emotional point of view however…" He stood completely still as though waiting for a judge to deliver his sentence. "I think there is every benefit to it. What you said earlier…no man has ever made me feel as cherished or as appreciated as you, my lord."

"You must call me Arthur."

"Must I?"

Pulling her back into his arms, he murmured against her lips, "I absolutely insist upon it," right before kissing her once again, this time with more joy in his heart than he'd ever felt before.

CHAPTER SEVENTEEN

"Are you sure you've searched in that direction?" Laura asked Fiona. Having agreed to help her sister find the elusive Thorncliff treasure, she'd ventured into the tunnels below the manor together with Milton, Rachel, Belgrave, Montsmouth, Emily, and Chadwick.

"Quite," Fiona stated with certainty. She looked toward Chadwick, who held one of the four lanterns they'd brought along. "Am I not correct?"

"You are," he said as he swung the light around. After following the tunnel he and Fiona had been exploring the previous day, they'd arrived at a cross section.

"Shall we split up then?" Laura asked. "Emily and Montsmouth could come with me and Lamont."

"It will be more efficient than all of us going the same way," Rachel said, while Belgrave nodded. After announcing their betrothal at breakfast, the earl had taken every opportunity to dote on his fiancée, while Rachel herself had smiled a lot more than usual.

Laura could not be more pleased. Even though she and Milton had not yet made a public announcement, she was thrilled to know Rachel, who'd been least likely to marry, had managed to find both love and happiness.

And then there was Emily and Montsmouth – a couple Laura still had to get used to, though Emily's assurance he was everything she'd ever hoped for offered more than enough reassurance. And although they had only just made their courtship known, Laura was certain they would soon be announcing their engagement, if the tender looks they were sending each other were any indication.

"Come on then," Montsmouth said. He started down the tunnel to the left.

"See you later," Fiona called. She hurried after Chadwick with Rachel and Belgrave in quick pursuit.

"After you." Milton pressed his palm against Laura's back. The depth of his voice lent a rich warmth that seemed to ward off the damp chill of the tunnel.

Starting after her sister and Montsmouth, Laura remained aware of Milton's solid presence behind her. He was a tall man with broad shoulders and a firm chest with hardened planes that bore evidence of an active lifestyle. As a woman who'd spent the greater part of her life imagining what her perfect hero might look like, she had to admit Milton was as close to perfection as she might have wished. In fact, she'd considered him at great length for some time – long before she'd ever imagined forming an attachment to him herself.

Inclined to admit her secret, she allowed Emily and Montsmouth to move on a few paces so they wouldn't hear what was only meant for Milton's ears. "You ought to know I've admired you for some time."

There was a slight moment of silence, and then a quietly murmured, "Really?" He sounded intrigued.

"When I started working on my first novel—"

"The one you recently published?"

"No. The one to which I am referring has never been read by anyone." She continued forward, carefully watching her footsteps while she went. The ground felt lumpy beneath her feet, with stones occasionally sticking up in a way that made her trip at least once. Milton caught her by the elbow with a steadying hand. "It features a woman who flees her mean-spirited guardian."

"The best stories do have a heavy dose of drama."

"I absolutely agree," Laura said. "And in this case, it offered the perfect opening for the hero to come to the rescue." Milton chuckled so deeply, she felt the vibrations flowing through her. Had they been completely alone... She forced herself to focus on what she'd been saying. "I wanted him to be strong – tall with broad shoulders and dashingly handsome. At the time, I didn't know anyone perfect enough to offer inspiration. Nobody really fit the image I had in my mind. Until I attended the Jupiter ball and saw you."

He was suddenly closer than before – so close she could feel his breath fanning across her neck. His hand clasped her shoulder, and his lips grazed her ear when he leaned forward to whisper, "And then?"

She could scarcely speak for the jittery nerves now bubbling up inside her. He'd lit her whole body on fire with that simple question. Against the tightening of her bodice, her heart drummed a rapid beat, the effect so intoxicating it made her feel slightly faint. "And then I had my inspiration for every hero I've written since."

His teeth scraped the side of her neck in a playful caress that made stars spark behind her eyes. "You drive me to distraction, Laura."

Shivering slightly, she whispered back, "I cannot wait for us to be wed – the sooner we make our engagement known, the better."

"I couldn't agree more." He'd leaned back again, adding some respectable distance, but not without letting his hand slide down her side and over her thigh.

Heavens, she'd never have thought a man might provoke such intense sensations inside her – that he might make her want things no decent woman had any business wanting. She'd probably have to broach the subject with him at some point. After all, she did hope to base her marriage on honesty.

"There's another intersection here," Emily said from further ahead.

Laura approached, with Milton right behind her. "I wonder if we'll ever find the end of these tunnels."

"Shall we split up again?" Montsmouth asked. "We can give ourselves half an hour and then meet back here. Do you have your pocket watch with you, Lamont?"

"I do." He pulled it out and checked the time. "It's three o'clock right now."

"Good. We'll meet you back here at half past three. Does that sound reasonable?" Montsmouth looked from Laura to Milton and back again.

"I believe so," Laura said with a glance toward her sister. There was no missing the hopeful gleam in her eyes or the color that rose to her cheeks. No doubt she was as eager to be alone with Montsmouth as Laura was to have Milton for herself.

"Then it's settled," Montsmouth said. Moving away from Laura and Milton, he guided Emily down the tunnel to the left.

The glow from his lantern diminished as they went, leaving Laura and Milton with considerably less light than before. "Allow me to lead the way." He stepped in front of her and started walking.

"I don't suppose you were counting on such an adventure when you decided to visit Thorncliff for Christmas."

He glanced at her over his shoulder, the planes of his face cast in dark relief and his eyes so black she could not make them out. "I didn't count on a lot of things, but I had my hopes. This adventure, as you call it, will be an interesting tale for us to tell our children one day."

The mention of starting a family together made Laura's toes curl with pleasure. "I never dared hope I would—" The sound of grating rock cut her off, and she instinctively leapt toward Milton who pulled her aside and away from a wall that slid into place, blocking their way back. Laura stared at it for a long moment before glancing down at the ground. "We must have triggered something."

"I felt a sinking movement beneath my foot right before it happened." He stomped around a bit, testing the ground. "It's right here, but I don't see a way to reverse the effect."

"It probably has to be done from the other side of that wall."

"Or perhaps there was no plan to reverse anything – perhaps this was meant to safeguard the treasure."

"That would mean it has to be somewhere back the way we came." Laura had never felt more deflated. "Our hope of finding it now is close to nil if your hypothesis is true."

"Agreed, though there is still a chance of your siblings finding it."

She expelled a deep breath. "We won't even be able to meet Emily and Montsmouth at the designated time."

"No. We've no choice but to continue in this direction and hope we find a way out."

Laura suddenly felt less brave than she had done when they'd all agreed to explore the Thorncliff foundations. "Do you suppose we might have some trouble with that?"

Taking her by the hand, Milton started off at a moderate pace. "No, but whether or not we do before this lantern runs out of fuel depends on the length of this tunnel. If I may, I'd like to suggest we make haste."

Agreeing with his logic, Laura gathered up the hem of her gown so she could walk faster. The air was musty and damp with a hint of dirt clinging to it that prompted her to cough every couple of minutes.

"I cannot wait to return upstairs for a cup of hot tea." In spite of the spencer and shawl she'd brought with her, she could feel the chilly air ripping through every layer of fabric and sinking its fangs into her skin.

Milton drew to a halt, set down the lantern, and began shrugging out of his jacket. "Here," he told her. He set the heavy garment over her shoulders. His warmth still clung to the fabric, infusing her with the heat she needed.

Still, she could not allow him to suffer on her account. "No. I couldn't possibly. You'll catch a cold or worse."

"Better me than you," he said in a tone that brooked no argument. Snatching up the lantern once more, he recommenced walking. "Look there. Do you see that?"

She didn't see anything at all since his much larger size blocked most of her view. "What is it?"

"Looks like a door."

Hope brimmed inside her. She no longer cared about finding the treasure. Her feet hurt, Milton was likely freezing, and with their way back blocked, her only interest at present was in finding some means of escape as quickly as possible. If there was a door, then they might have found an alternate route.

"It's locked," Milton said, shortly after he'd tried to first pull, then push on the handle. He held the lantern toward Laura. "Hold this please and step back a bit."

She did so without question, watching silently while Milton threw his right shoulder against the door once, twice, three times. It finally splintered beneath his weight in an impressive show of masculine strength and power. Laura stared at the bits of wood that lay strewn around and at those still hanging from the hinges.

"Most of it was rotted." He rubbed his shoulder for a moment before taking the lantern from her hand. "Breaking it down would have been a lot harder otherwise."

"I still find your efforts incredibly admirable." Of course, she couldn't seem to tear her eyes away from his chest or from his arms. The muscles there were far more apparent now that he'd taken off his jacket, and the sight made Laura long for more contact between them – for him to hold her close so she could revel in the security he was capable of providing.

Meeting her gaze, he paused for one second before muttering something beneath his breath and heading through the now open doorway. She followed him into a large circular room with a spiral staircase built out of stone. Milton took a turn of the space with the lantern. "It looks as though the only way for us to go is up," he said.

"Do you think this might be a remnant from the original manor? Spencer says it was built by a knight in the twelfth century."

"Judging from the way the stones are laid – the style of masonry, that is – I'd say this stairwell is quite a lot older than other parts of the manor. The themed salons, for instance, were probably built a couple of centuries ago. But the interior courtyard which sits to the west of the foyer and some of the hallways there share a medieval look."

"The ballroom doesn't, and that room is right off the courtyard."

"Lady Duncaster has said the manor has undergone many renovations – most recently under her own supervision. To dress a room with polished wood flooring, mirrors, and stucco would not have been difficult."

"And it would have transformed it tremendously."

He smiled in response, then turned toward the stairs and allowed the glow from his lantern to light the first steps. "Shall we see where this leads?"

Nodding, she followed him up slowly until they arrived at a wide landing which didn't appear to have any doors. Instead, a large square piece of glass had been set into the stone roughly four feet off the ground. Milton held his lantern toward it and Laura stepped up beside him for a closer look. "Is that—"

"Lord Duncaster's study," Milton said with as much awe as Laura felt. "This has to be the mirror above the fireplace."

"Do you think there's a way to get in there from here?"

Milton shifted the lantern, holding it as close as possible to the wall so the light could spill across the uneven surface of crudely shaped bricks.

"There," Laura said with a sudden sense of excitement when she glimpsed a slight anomaly in the structure. "Go back. A bit more. Yes. Right there. What is that?"

Milton peered down at the brick Laura was pointing toward. "It looks as if something's been etched into it…letters or numbers perhaps?"

Laura leaned in as well and allowed her fingers to trail across the rough indentations. "I think this might be an N followed by a C…no, there's another line here. It has to be an E and a…" She frowned as she tried to make sense of the squiggly letter. "I don't know, but the last one looks like an S, so perhaps the one I can't figure out is a W?" Leaning back, she met Milton's gaze. "It would make sense with the references my siblings found to North, South, East and West, both in my grandfather's notes and the letter my great aunt sent from France."

"They decided to leave their mark, though I suspect there may be more to it than that." Reaching out, he placed the palm of his hand against the brick and pushed.

The wall creaked before starting to turn with a grating sound while dust spilled from every crack. Laura stared at the opening it formed. She could see the fireplace molding now as it stood sideways, allowing for passage on either side. "Shall I go first?"

"Please do," Milton said. Stepping forward, he lowered the lantern to light her way before following.

Laura scrambled out into the study on her hands and knees, her foot catching on the hem of her gown and causing her to fall forward. She immediately rolled onto her back and sat up.

"Are you all right?" Milton asked, coming to kneel by her side. He'd set the lantern down and placed his hand against her cheek. A frown crinkled his forehead, while concern flooded his eyes. "Did you hurt yourself?"

"No." Laura leaned against his touch, reveling in the feel of his skin and the warmth he emitted. Placing her palms on the carpet behind her, she leaned back on her arms and tipped up her chin. "I am fine." She couldn't quite stop herself from dropping her gaze to his lips and admiring their fullness. Her own felt suddenly dry, so she licked them, aware he followed the movement with a dark sort of interest that instantly tightened her limbs.

He leaned forward, paused long enough to allow their breaths to mingle, and then pressed his mouth to hers with an urgency that pushed her off balance. Her hands slid outward, and she was suddenly on her back with his much larger body pinning her down to the floor. His lips were moving against hers while his hands slid scandalously against her thigh, her waist, the side of her breast. She moaned, deep and throaty, as she gave herself up to his kiss and to every sensation he was trying to bestow. She tasted toffee, nuts, and chocolate…a hint of coffee too. The flavor was more than divine, it was intoxicating.

He pressed himself closer, kissing her fully and deeply until he groaned with a pleasure that heated her skin and tightened her belly. Her arms wound their way around him, hugging him close while she arched up against him, her skirts a tangled mess around her knees…knees he suddenly touched with his hand…a hand sliding gradually higher. "Yes… Please…"

The door to the study burst open, and Milton cursed as he threw himself off her and pulled down her skirts. Light flooded the space, and Laura sat up, blinking past locks of stray hair that had come undone from her coiffure to fall across her forehead.

"Well. If this isn't a compromising situation, I don't know what is," came Lady Duncaster's voice.

"I can explain," Milton said, now helping Laura to rise so she could appreciate the true awfulness of the situation. Because Lady Duncaster wasn't alone. Laura's mother and father stood by the countess's side, both staring at Laura and Milton with grim expressions.

"I look forward to hearing every word," Lord Oakland remarked.

"We are affianced," Laura blurted. The last thing she wanted was for Milton to have to endure her father's wrath. "You may offer your congratulations."

It was as if dark thunderclouds cleared, and the sun came shining through. "Well," Laura's mother exclaimed with a smile of pleasure completely apart from her previous expression of horror. She stepped forward, as did Lord Oakland, whose sudden grin was hard to fathom.

He shook Milton's hand. "Welcome to the family."

"We couldn't be more pleased," Lady Oakland added.

"I don't know what to say," Milton said. He sounded as stunned as Laura felt. But a quick glance in Lady Duncaster's direction suggested that maybe this match had not been as accidental as Laura might have believed. She didn't care. The most important thing of all was she'd found a man who was certain to love her as much as she would love him. And nothing in the world had ever felt more right than that.

CHAPTER EIGHTEEN

"DID YOU HEAR THAT?" EMILY turned to stare back along the tunnel through which they'd been walking.

"It sounded like heavy blocks of stone moving across the ground," Charles muttered. Stepping closer to Emily, he took hold of her hand. "That can't be possible, though. Can it?"

She shook her head. "I wouldn't think so."

"Come on then." He carefully pulled her along with him. "Let's see where this leads so we can get out of here."

"You're not much of an adventurer are you?"

He slanted a look in her direction. "No. I prefer clean parlors to filthy underground passageways." Wrinkling his nose he added, "It smells like someone died down here."

That comment quickened her pace. "Do you really think so?"

"No, but I'm sure there must be rats and other unsavory creatures."

Shuddering, she clasped his hand more tightly. "My brother mentioned bats when he ventured into the cavern."

"Well, there you are then – bats are flying rats, are they not?"

"They're certainly not pleasant," she muttered. Oh, if only she hadn't allowed Fiona to convince her to venture into this subterranean maze. "I'm sorry I got you into this mess."

He swung around, facing her with a stormy expression that managed to do all sorts of curious things to her insides. "There's no need for you to apologize, Emily." He blew out a breath and took a step closer. "You're trying to help your sister realize a dream, and that's a noble cause if there ever was one. As for me, I shouldn't be complaining, considering the fact I started this search myself. Granted, I always thought the treasure would be in some closedoff and forgotten room above stairs, or at least in a proper cellar. Still, I would like to find it as much as Fiona would, perhaps even more."

Emily chuckled, "I doubt *more* would be possible. That jewelry box is all Fiona thinks about these days."

"And finding the missing paintings was all I could think about until you began occupying my mind." He held up the lantern, illuminating their faces, and she could see he was smiling in a way she'd never seen him do before, with deep satisfaction. "Considering my grandfather's role in all of this, as dishonorable as it may have been, finding those paintings is still important to me. But it is not as important as it once was. You matter more now, so if you would rather abandon this search, you need only say the word, and I shall return upstairs with you for a glass of mulled wine or a walk in the snow – your choice."

Laura stared at him, at how the light caught the darker flecks of bronze in his eyes and made them shine like liquid caramel. He was willing to give up his quest for her, and while she appreciated the sentiment, she could not let him do it. "No." Reaching out, she took him by the hand. "Let us see this through together." Because not doing so might make him resent her one day, whether he wished to or not, and that was something she would not be able to bear. And besides…"How often does the chance to search for treasure on a mysterious estate come along in one lifetime? We would have to be fools to pass it up."

His smile broadened. "This is what I love about you."

"What you ah…er…*love* about me?"

"Your kind and selfless heart," he explained. The smile faded, and he turned quite serious. "Besides being the most incredible artist I have ever met—"

"You flatter me too much." She couldn't possibly be the *most* talented.

"I say what I truly think, Emily." Lowering his head, he placed a kiss upon her forehead before whispering against her skin, "And the truth is, you are lovelier than any other woman I have ever known. To have won your affection has humbled me in ways you cannot possibly imagine." He kissed her again. This time, his lips lingered for an extra second before he quietly added, "I know we spoke of courtship, but you should know my mind is already set. You are all I need, all I will ever desire, which is why my greatest hope now is to secure your hand in marriage."

Inhaling sharply, she tightened her hold on his

hand. "Charles."

The name was but a breath of air as she raised her face toward his. Seeking his lips, she secured a kiss wrought from love and admiration, pleasure and need. She kissed him slowly, allowing every possible sensation, each touch, to imprint itself on her mind. Releasing his hand, she curled her fingers around his lapels and held him to her, so close she could feel the beat of his heart matching hers through all the layers of fabric between them.

"Yes," she murmured against his mouth. "Yes, I will marry you."

No sooner had she spoken the words than she felt herself wrapped in his embrace. His lips molded against hers in a kiss more demanding than any they'd shared before. It took and gave in equal measure, drawing them closer and forging a bond that Emily knew could never be broken. It left her feeling both hopeful and breathless as she stood in the chilly murkiness, reveling in the warmth that flowed between her and Charles, the strength he exuded while he held her like he never wanted to let her go.

"You will be mine." He spoke with incredulity tingeing his voice.

"I will be yours," she echoed. She liked the sound of that assurance.

The next kiss he gave her was hard and demanding. It swept aside all sweetness as he took possession in an elemental show of power that weakened her knees and quickened her heart. "If only we were anywhere but here," he growled low in her ear. "If only we were already wed. The things I would show you…"

Seduced by the deep timbre of his voice, she daringly asked, "What things?"

With a low growl he pushed her hips against his, so tight she could feel…dear God, she could actually feel…Words could not describe the fresh sensations spiraling through her, the heat that began to gather and the sudden need to be touched in a way she'd never been touched before. A gasp was all she could offer in response. More so when he whispered against her ear, his breath caressing her skin in a way that inflamed her soul. "I would show you what it means to be touched by a man whose thirst for you is unquenchable. I would lay you bare and show you pleasure unlike any you've ever experienced before."

"Heaven!"

He chuckled darkly. "I will show you that as well." Drawing back, he held up the lantern and studied her face. His eyes met hers, full of promise and sin. "But first, we have a task to complete. The quicker the better, if you ask me."

Agreeing with him, Emily let him lead the way along the tunnel while doing her best to suppress the feelings he'd stirred in her. He would lay her bare, he'd said, and she suddenly had a vision of herself spread out upon his bed like some pagan offering while he devoured her with his gaze. The notion was both exciting and frightening. She'd never been completely naked in front of anyone before – not since she'd been a child – and the thought she would be so soon, in front of him, filled her with trepidation.

What if she didn't live up to his expectations? What if he found her lacking somehow? She wasn't sure what she'd imagined from marriage, but oddly, the idea of taking her clothes off in front of her husband had never entered her mind. It did now with full force as she reflected on her thighs and her belly. Perhaps they could be trimmer? And then there were her breasts. They suddenly seemed the wrong size.

Ten minutes later, she'd convinced herself she was going to be an immense disappointment. After all, considering his expectations and the obvious admiration he felt for her, there was no other possible outcome. Which only increased her concerns for the wedding they would have, and the first night they would share together as husband and wife.

"You've gone really quiet," Charles murmured after another five minutes. "Is everything all right?"

She could lie, but the truth would likely serve her better no matter how awkward confessing her thoughts would be. "I worry you will find me lacking."

"Lacking? How so?"

"You know…" How could she possibly bring herself to say it?

"No. I really don't," he said, leading her around a curved corner.

Catching him by the elbow, she drew him to a halt and stepped around him, blocking his path. She took a step back and bolstered her courage. "When I take my clothes off," she explained, "and…and… you see what I look like without them."

His features softened with compassion. "Darling, I can promise you I will adore the way you look."

"How can you possibly be so sure?" She turned

and started walking, eager to spend the excess energy simmering through her. Somehow, she'd managed to put herself into a state of panic.

"Emily. You have to trust me in this."

She could hear his footsteps closing in on her. "But I—"

Her words were lost as the ground somehow opened up directly beneath her feet. She fell on a scream while her arms frantically reached for something to grab hold of – anything at all. Instead she was caught by her wrist so hard her body was yanked to one side. "I've got you," Charles grit between his teeth while pain tore its way through her shoulder.

"I…I… Oh God, please help me!" Her legs dangled beneath her while she tried to get a foothold.

"Stop moving," Charles said.

"I can't. I need to—"

"Listen to me," he told her calmly. "I will get you back up to the surface, but in order for that to happen, you have to help me. When you move, your weight shifts and holding you becomes harder, so please, do as I say and stay still."

As counterintuitive as it was, Emily gulped in some air, closed her eyes around the tears that were brimming, and followed Charles's instructions. She was very much aware that her heart might give out before she managed to fall to her death. Which she wouldn't. He'd given her his word, and she had to listen. "Very well."

Cursing beneath his breath, Charles reached for Emily's left arm and started pulling her up. The moment she'd fallen he'd flung himself forward, landing hard on his belly and shattering the lantern. The flame still burned by some miracle, but it was dimmer than before, affording him limited light. Shifting his hand from her right wrist to her elbow, he heard her gasp in pain and realized then she must have hurt herself when he'd initially caught her. *Bloody hell!* This should at least have been him, not her. He was supposed to go first. If he had, he would have lit the path and seen it gave way to a gaping hole.

Bracing his feet against the walls of the tunnel, he readjusted his hold on her left arm. She screamed then as her weight hinged on her right elbow. But he managed to catch her beneath her left armpit, increasing his leverage and quickening her ascent. "Grab onto me. Anywhere you can. Pull yourself up."

He felt her hands clawing against the back of his jacket, her fingers gripping and tugging the fabric while he reached for her right underarm and then for her waist. "Almost here," he assured her, doing his best to keep his voice level. Inside, his nerves had twisted into a chaotic mess. She grabbed his legs, and he caught her backside, hauling her the rest of the way until both of them were lying on the dirt and panting for breath. *Christ!* His chest felt sore.

Rolling onto his side, he moved to gather her up in his arms. "Emily." His arms came around her trembling body, and for a long moment, he simply held her while thanking the heavens she still lived.

"Thank you." Her voice shook.

When Charles moved to kiss her upon her

cheeks, he encountered the dampness of tears. So he kissed her eyes while soothing her with strokes up and down her spine. "Shhh…" he whispered between each kiss. "You're safe now."

Her breaths calmed, and she finally began to relax against him. "I'm sorry I went on without you. It was stupid of me." She started crying again. When the tears finally ceased, she quietly told him, "I almost lost the chance to experience everything you want to show me – all because I let fear divest me of my senses."

"The important thing is, you're still alive, but I think we may need a doctor to tend to your shoulder. I suspect it might be dislocated."

"It hurts like the devil," Emily admitted.

"Right then. I suggest we get you back upstairs with immediate haste." Squatting beside her, he grabbed the broken lantern and told her to hold it. She did as he asked, allowing him to lift her into his arms before setting off back the way they had come.

She lighted the way while nestling close against his chest. And although he could feel her warm body against him, he still couldn't help but consider what might have transpired if he had not been quick enough to catch her or strong enough to hold her. That thought made his whole body shudder with apprehension.

"I love you," he murmured against her hair. He quickened his pace with determination.

"I love you too," she whispered, her voice so sweet and gentle in spite of all she'd endured.

There was no doubt in his mind he was the most fortunate man in the world, and he would spend the remainder of his days proving that in every conceivable way.

CHAPTER NINETEEN

Arriving at her sister's bedchamber, Fiona knocked on the door and waited for it to open. It did so quickly enough, allowing Fiona to slip inside the comfortable space. It had been tastefully decorated in creamy tones and gold accents. Adding a hint of Christmas cheer, a bowl of pine cones scented with cinnamon had been placed on the table closest to the door, welcoming those who entered. Fiona breathed in the fragrant scent before carefully wrapping her arms around Emily. "I am so pleased to see you looking better." Pulling back, she met her gaze and told her sincerely, "We were all so worried about you."

"I was worried too while I was hanging over that awful abyss."

Fiona couldn't even begin to imagine. When she'd heard of Emily's ordeal, she'd hurried to see her immediately, only to be kept away by her parents and Montsmouth, who all insisted Emily needed to rest. "It must have been terrifying."

"It was." She gave a wistful smile. "Charles saved me though."

"So informal?" Fiona teased.

Emily blushed and her smile broadened. "He asked me to marry him, and I have accepted."

Fiona hugged her sister once more. "That's wonderful news! I wonder how nobody mentioned it."

"That part was my idea. I didn't want all the attention right after the incident, so I'm thinking we should wait until tonight before making a formal announcement."

"The ball will make for a perfect occasion," Fiona agreed. "I was actually wondering if you needed help dressing, but I see you managed quite well on your own. That gown looks stunning on you by the way."

"Thank you, Fiona. To be honest, I called for a maid to help, though I must confess my shoulder is working perfectly once more. Montsmouth made a fuss about it, however. He insisted I not strain it in any way, so I agreed to be coddled for his peace of mind."

"I've never seen a man more shaken than he," Fiona told her. "I believe he loves you a great deal."

"As I love him. Indeed, I consider myself the most fortunate of women, Fiona." An odd hint of sadness touched Emily's eyes before she quietly added, "It would be wonderful for you to experience the sort of joy I have found. Perhaps Chadwick—"

"No," Fiona said. "He has no interest in me. Not in that way, at least."

"I cannot believe that. Perhaps if—"

"Can we please forget about Chadwick and simply enjoy the evening without worrying about whether or not I will receive an offer too?" Taking Emily's hand, she gave it a little squeeze. "There is already plenty for us to celebrate with you, Laura, and Rachel taken into account." Fiona was enormously pleased with her sisters' good fortunes. "Mama and Papa must be beside themselves with joy."

"And you are still young, Fiona. You have plenty of time to become affianced and marry."

As optimistic as her sister's words were no doubt meant to be, they filled Fiona with a sense of depressing hopelessness. Yes, she had time, but not to make the right match. It seemed that doing so would now be impossible since the only man she wanted did not want her. "Are you ready to go down to the ballroom?" she asked in a joyful tone that sounded far too false and eager. "There will be other people present besides our own party. No doubt I shall find a handsome vicar with whom to dance."

Emily laughed and followed Fiona out of the room, her pale yellow gown twirling about her legs in an elegant way that was sure to draw attention. Fiona herself had chosen to wear a lilac creation with lace cap sleeves. As pointless as it would be, she'd hoped to draw Chadwick's attention since the low décolletage made it slightly more daring than anything else he'd ever seen her in. She huffed out a breath. He probably wouldn't even notice.

"We wanted to wait for you before heading in," Laura said when she met her and Emily at the foot of the grand staircase. She was standing together with Lamont and Montsmouth who immediately hurried to Emily's side and offered her his arm. "Rachel and Belgrave are keeping company with a scientist Lady Duncaster invited – some gentleman by the name of Sir David Brewster. I have a feeling they will be happily occupied by him for the remainder of the evening."

"Lucky Rachel," Fiona said, falling into step next to Laura while Lamont followed behind. Glancing up, she caught sight of the garlands that hung on the walls. The scarlet bows adorning them offered a pretty contrast to the dark green pine, and as she inhaled, she caught a breath of the trees from which they'd been cut. It reminded her of the game of hideandgoseek she'd played with Chadwick a week and a half ago. It had been silly and fun until everything had somehow managed to change. They no longer laughed together as they once had, and she found she longed to do so again more than she longed for him to reciprocate her love.

"You look incredible tonight," Laura whispered while they walked.

Feeling a blush creep into her cheeks, Fiona wondered if perhaps she'd made a mistake with her gown. It made her feel horribly self-conscious all of a sudden. "You sound surprised."

"Only because I have made a bad habit of thinking of you as my little sister – the girl who used to chase me with sticky marmalade fingers when we were children. I tend to forget you're all grown up now – a diamond of the first water with every chance of making an excellent match for yourself."

"I have no such intention this evening," Fiona said. They entered the ballroom where light shimmered from the crystal chandeliers overhead while music rose in waves of melodic pleasure. Red velvet bows strung with tiny bells had been pinned along the walls in a festive display of holiday cheer.

Sucking in a breath, Fiona admired the efforts Lady Duncaster and her servants had gone to for the sake of one evening. "Oh, isn't this lovely?"

"It is indeed," Laura said, while Emily and Montsmouth slipped passed them and headed toward the dance floor. Lamont moved closer to Laura's side.

"May I introduce Mr. Haroldson, Mr. Brown, and Mr. Danton?" Lady Duncaster asked. She'd approached with the three young gentlemen in tow, each more eager-looking than the other.

"Delighted," Fiona said.

"I take it you live in these parts?" Lamont asked.

"My family owns land half an hour west of here," Mr. Haroldson said. He was the slimmest of the bunch and in possession of a pleasant expression that compensated nicely for what he lacked in looks.

Mr. Brown nodded. "I inherited an estate a couple of years ago. It used to specialize in agriculture, but I find fishing to be a far more profitable source of income. And with the shore as close as it is, there is some convenience to it. I've about twenty vessels that go out every morning. The catch is then shipped off to the markets in London."

"How admirable," Fiona said. She was rewarded with a smile that made Mr. Brown appear both appreciative and handsome at the same time. "And what of you, Mr. Danton?" She gave her attention to the last gentleman. He'd held back, making him appear humbler than the other two.

"I got my law degree from Cambridge three years ago and have since set up a small office in the village. People travel from both near and far in order to consult me, and the rent is cheaper than anything I might be able to find in London." Mr. Danton met Fiona's gaze with directness. "It provides me with a comfortable home and a reasonable income."

"Mr. Danton has done really well for himself," Lady Duncaster said, like a mother hen trying to show off her chick. "Most would consider a house with twenty rooms a manor, but he is far too modest to make a show of his accomplishments. So I must take it upon myself to do it for him."

Mr. Danton smiled tightly. "I shouldn't think a label would matter."

Lady Duncaster laughed. "Oh indeed, you are quite mistaken there, Mr. Danton. Unfortunately our society is built exclusively upon labels – more precisely, the *right* ones."

"Which is why titles hold such great value," Mr. Haroldson pointed out. He took a small step toward Fiona. "If I may, I would like to request a dance from you."

Fiona dutifully pulled out her dance card and offered it to him. Mr. Brown glanced at Laura, prompting Lamont to say, "If you will excuse us, I believe the quadrille is starting, and I have promised Lady Laura I would dance it with her." With a bow, he then guided Laura away from the group.

Fiona managed to catch a murmured, "sorry," from her sister before she disappeared into the crowd. Lady Duncaster extricated herself soon after, leaving Fiona alone with her new admirers. She accepted a dance from Mr. Brown and Mr. Danton as well and agreed to join them for some refreshment while they waited for the next set to begin.

"Would you care for some cake?" Mr. Haroldson asked. He indicated the beautiful creations the cook had made for the occasion. One contained nuts and berries, while one had been made from decadent chocolate. The third, which Fiona selected, was a vanilla layer cake with custard in the middle. All had been covered in thick blue frosting and decorated with white marzipan snowflakes.

"Some champagne to go with it?" Mr. Brown offered, while Mr. Danton provided Fiona with a napkin.

"Only if you will have some as well," she told the trio, who were almost falling over each other in their efforts to see to her every need. When they hesitated, she added a distinct, "I insist." Upon which more glasses were swiftly filled with the bubbly liquid.

As expected, the cake was divine. Fiona happily ate every last crumb of it while listening as attentively as possible to what her companions were saying. One spoke of farmland, the other about mackerel and pollock, and the third about a legal dispute between two shop owners.

Glancing around, Fiona scanned the room. Her parents conversed with an elderly couple on the far side, while Rachel and Belgrave kept company with a white-haired gentleman who had to be in possession of the bushiest whiskers Fiona had ever seen. She supposed he must be Sir David Brewster.

Sliding her gaze to the left, she located Emily and Montsmouth and Laura and Lamont. All four were engaged in the quadrille, as was…Fiona blinked… Chadwick. With laughing eyes and his typical boyish grin, he guided his dance partner about the floor with remarkable elegance.

Fiona's mouth went dry. Her stomach tightened, and something unpleasant began to take root in her chest. She had no right to be jealous of the pretty young woman with whom he was dancing, yet it was almost as if she could scarcely breathe. A knot had formed in her throat, and she suddenly felt impossibly cold.

"My lady?"

She turned in the direction of the voice that had spoken and found all three gentlemen staring back at her in question.

"Are you all right?" Mr. Danton inquired.

"You look a bit pale," Mr. Haroldson said.

"Perhaps you would like to sit?" Mr. Brown suggested.

All Fiona wanted to do was flee. It hadn't occurred to her until this precise moment that seeing Chadwick dance with another woman could have such a jarring effect. She actually wanted to push his lovely dance partner away from him! But what purpose would that have other than convincing Chadwick she was an absolute lunatic?

So she blew out a breath and squared her shoulders, ignored the pain that twisted inside her, and pasted a deliberate smile upon her face. "I am perfectly well, gentlemen. No need for concern."

They couldn't have looked more relieved, and as the quadrille drew to a close, Fiona found herself whisked off to the dance floor by Mr. Haroldson. She danced a reel and a country dance next before ending up with Mr. Haroldson once more for a minute.

"I simply couldn't resist," he told her, looking tremendously pleased with himself. "To find a lady as lovely as yourself in these parts is a rarity. Tell me," he murmured while he led her about, "might I call on you here tomorrow? We could take a carriage ride together and stop for tea and cake somewhere. I could show you my property, if you like."

Sensing the direction in which this was going, Fiona took a moment to consider her response to him properly. "You are exceptionally kind to offer me such attention. Please know I am most appreciative, but it would be wrong of me not to tell you that my affection lies elsewhere."

"Well then," he said. It took a second for him to continue. "I thank you for your candor, my lady. The man who has claimed your heart is fortunate indeed."

Fiona valued the sentiment, even though the man in question would never be made aware of her feelings for him – not when she knew his feelings for her were only platonic. Revealing the contents of her heart would probably kill her, but she managed to nod in agreement and finished her dance with a smile. They parted ways then, and she set out to find her parents. If she kept their company for the remainder of the evening, or engaged in a game of cards perhaps, then she might be able to distract herself from the fact she was the only remaining sibling to yet make a match – that she was alone and that her heart had been broken.

But when she made her way along the periphery of the ballroom, accepting two more dances as she went, she found her path blocked by none other than the man whom she sought to avoid. Because as fate would have it, Chadwick stepped right in front of her, and as luck would have it, he was more dashing than ever before. It didn't seem possible, and yet it was. Fiona wanted to scream with frustration or at least stomp her foot. Instead, she did her best to appear unaffected, even though she felt weak-kneed and wobbly.

"There you are," she managed to say. "I was beginning to wonder where you were." Feigning indifference had never come easily to her, but she made her best attempt at doing so now in order to keep her pride intact.

"Fiona." His eyes held a stormy gleam that made her want to leap straight into his arms. Tamping down the temptation, she held back while he looked her over. Whatever emotion he'd initially shown upon seeing her was immediately banked behind layers of cool reserve that did nothing but tear her soul to shreds. He took her hand and bowed over it, kissing the air above her knuckles before straightening once again.

"How can it be you've managed to outshine all other women this evening?"

She felt an immediate rush of heat and knew she must be blushing. "It has to be my feminine charm," she said, with an overstated emphasis on the word *charm*.

He smiled in response to that with such genuineness, Fiona felt something lift from her shoulders. Unable to stop herself, she grinned, and soon he was grinning as well. It felt remarkably good and… normal…as if the world was finally spinning in the right direction again.

"I actually wondered if you would like to dance with me tonight." He sounded almost shy, which she found a little bit odd. Chadwick had always been the most self-assured individual of her acquaintance, especially when they were together. For him to sound uncertain now made her feel slightly wary, perhaps even a bit uncomfortable.

She drew a breath. *No. It isn't safe. You won't survive it,* an inner voice warned her. But then another more tempting voice beckoned, *Yes, please. Let me pretend for a little while and pick up the pieces of my broken heart tomorrow.* She chose to listen to the latter and held her dance card toward him. "We never have before. I think it might be about time."

His face tightened, and his smile gradually dimmed until it was barely visible at all. Slowly, as if he might be regretting his suggestion, he took the dance card, studied it for what seemed an eternity, and finally scribbled his name. "There you are," he said when he handed the card back.

Curious, Fiona dropped her gaze and stared at the spot where his bold letters had been written. "The waltz?" She should have heeded that first voice instead, because this was going to be torture. A thought popped into her head. "I've yet to be granted permission to dance it."

He merely shrugged. "That rule applies mainly to Almack's and its patronesses, none of whom are here."

"True, but there are still my parents to consider."

"You think they might disapprove?" He gave a thoughtful nod. "They might. We can ask for their permission."

"But—"

"Unless, of course, you wish to avoid waltzing with me for some reason?" His brows knit, and he searched her face for some sign of reluctance. Which she would then have to explain.

Oh, darn it!

"Of course not." Her voice was too high pitched to sound even remotely normal. She forced her best smile. "Waltzing with you will be so much fun, Chadwick. I can scarcely wait!"

Perfect! Now he looked suspicious!

Deciding to distract him from her peculiar behavior, she grabbed him by his hand and started leading him through the crowd, which made several people turn and stare. Too agitated to care, Fiona chose to ignore them while she spoke to Chadwick over her shoulder. "Let us settle this now then, shall we? I believe my parents are right over there."

CHAPTER TWENTY

ON ONE HAND, EDWARD LIKED the spontaneity with which Fiona had taken him by the hand. Such an act was not generally seen in a ballroom — or anywhere else for that matter — which was probably why they met with so many frowns of disapproval as they made their way through the crowd. But on the other hand, a part of him felt compelled to pull his hand away and deny himself the harrowing bliss he found from such simple contact. Both were wearing gloves, yet he could feel not only the warmth of her body permeating the thin fabric but the beat of her pulse whenever their wrists happened to meet, the strength of her fingers wound around his.

She did not want to dance with him, that much was clear. Her reluctance when he'd made the suggestion could not have been plainer. The question was why. When he'd tried to broach her averseness, she'd quickly denied it while doing her best to look as agreeable as possible. The act hadn't fooled him for a second, but it had torn at his heart.

Trying to conjure some explanation for her response, the only thing he could think was that she might have guessed how he felt about her – that perhaps, somehow, no matter how careful he'd been, he'd given himself away – and that now she was trying to add some distance in the hope he might withdraw his affection. He could never do so. A heart was not so easily ordered about. But maybe he could do better at this game of pretense he'd been playing ever since she'd made her lack of interest known. He drew a deep breath as they came to a halt before Lord and Lady Oakland and greeted them both in turn.

"Chadwick has asked me to dance the waltz with him," Fiona blurted. Ordinarily, her lack of finesse would have made him laugh – it always had – but tonight it pushed at the wound covering his soul.

"Fiona thought it proper for us to obtain your permission first," Chadwick explained when Lord Oakland directed a pair of raised eyebrows at him. "I quite agree."

"Well, I…er…hmmm…" Lady Oakland waved her fan with rapid beats. "I certainly have no objection to it."

Fiona stared. "But—"

"Nor do I," Lord Oakland muttered, much to Edward's surprise. After the last reprimand, he would have expected some argument at least. Instead, the earl now seemed positively determined. His jaw was set, and his eyes held a gleam to them as if to say, "Well, what are you going to do about this?"

"Mama," Fiona's voice had shrunk to a tiny whisper.

"You are like family, Chadwick. I hardly think it would be any worse than if she were to dance that particular dance with one of her brothers." There was something about Lady Oakland's mouth as she spoke – something telling – like a smile that was being forced back.

Edward stared at the people who had been like a second set of parents for him growing up. "Excellent," he managed to say, and then, to test his rising suspicions... "Might I also take her for a walk in the garden afterward? With the sun out today, much of the snow will have melted."

Fiona spun toward him faster than a weathervane changing direction in a storm.

"As long as she takes a shawl with her, I see no issue," Lady Oakland said. Her smile finally rose to the surface.

"I agree with my wife," Lord Oakland said, and then he winked.

Edward could not have been more stunned if the man had hit him over the head with a mallet, because something had suddenly been made quite clear – the earl and countess had given Edward their blessing to pursue their daughter with the prospect of marrying her. They did, after all, know him well enough not to worry about him ever casting her aside after a kiss. He would do right by her, and their expressions bore testament to that.

If only Fiona were equally agreeable. Instead, she appeared as rigid as a rock where she stood. Her lips were slightly parted while she stared at her parents with what could only be deemed complete and utter horror. Well, if there was a way for him to have his confidence stripped away completely, she'd certainly found the means to do it.

He offered her his arm. "Shall we?"

She gave him a dutiful nod – the sort that made him want to shake her until she returned to being the young and carefree woman he'd fallen in love with. Especially because he knew she cared for him, and while it might not be in the way he hoped, dancing with him could surely not be so bad as to make her react like this. Could it?

Deciding to broach the issue again, he quietly asked while they walked away from her parents, "Have I done something to upset you in any way?"

Her head tipped up at him in surprise. "No. Of course not. Why would you think that?"

"Because it appears you would rather be anywhere else but in my company. At the very least, you don't seem to care for waltzing with me."

"Oh." She bit her lip in that adorable way she always did whenever she felt chastised. They arrived at the dance floor where a reel was still underway. "I am sorry," she whispered, so low he scarcely heard her. "I…I have not felt quite like myself lately."

"Since coming here?" Bored with watching the reel, he dropped a look in her direction. "Or more precisely, since our snowball fight?" He noticed she'd gone completely still, which was unusual in its own way since Fiona was always so animated, even when doing nothing but standing upright. There was always a gentle sway to her or a tapping foot or fidgeting fingers. Right now, there was nothing. It was as if a gust of arctic air had blown into the ballroom and frozen her in place. "Fiona?"

Carefully, as though she feared she might break if she moved too quickly, she finally turned to meet his gaze. Edward stared at the stormy emotions swirling in the depths of her dark green eyes. He couldn't discern their meaning, but he knew it was far more important than she was letting on – that there was more to this strange distance between them than her not feeling like herself lately.

"I feel as though something is changing between us, Edward."

His chest tightened, both from the implication of her words and from the familiar use of his name. One made him feel as though he was falling away from her while the other seemed to anchor him in place. "You have grown up, Fiona," he told her simply, or as simply as he could without letting her know how aware he was of the fact. "We cannot continue to play as we once did when you were a young girl with braided hair and grass-stained skirts."

Chuckling, she nudged his shoulder in a way that reminded him of warm summer days and the greenest grass he'd ever seen set against vivid displays of flowers and golden sunshine. Damn, how he missed those days – how he wished he'd cherished them more. They had all passed by in the blink of an eye, and now he was here, in love with the woman the girl had become and still missing the girl in some sentimental muck-up that seemed impossible for him to untangle.

"I was quite the brat, as I recall." There was a hint of mischief in her voice that instantly warmed his heart.

"All you ever wanted was to be challenged." He spoke the words without even thinking, proving how well he knew her. Because when he considered what he'd said, he became increasingly aware of how perfectly those words defined her.

The reel ended and a new tune started up – the waltz, this time. Offering Fiona his arm, Edward led her out onto the floor and carefully turned her toward him. One hand clasped hers while the other settled gently against her lower back. And just like that, he found himself incapable of speech. Because it took every ounce of concentration he possessed to refrain from displaying the elemental need that surged through his veins in response to such simple contact. But oh, there was nothing simple about it, was there? She wanted nothing more than for them to go back to the way things had been when they'd climbed trees together and gotten their feet muddy in puddles. He, on the other hand, wished to move forward, to explore something more, something she probably didn't even know could exist between a man and a woman.

So he gritted his teeth and began counting backward even when the waltz moved them forward. Perhaps he should have listened when she'd tried to avoid this particular dance. But he'd been stubbornly determined to have at least this, if nothing else. He'd wanted to know what it might be like to hold her close and pretend for a while – before he forced himself to walk away from her forever. Well, perhaps not forever, but for as long as he'd need in order to forget how much he loved her and how much it would pain him to see her with someone else. Wincing, he spun her around the edge of the dance floor. Forever would not grant him enough time for such a feat. Nothing would.

"Did I step on your toes?"

He did his best to adjust his brain to the time and

place he was presently in. "What?"

"You winced, so I thought perhaps..?" A question loomed in her eyes.

"No." He forced a smile from somewhere deep down inside, one founded on a memory of her in a field of clover two summers ago. A group of swallows had been chasing each other across the sky, and the sight of it had brought so much joy to Fiona, it had been impossible for him not to feel joy as well. It was one of the things he loved about her – her infectious good cheer. "In fact," he said, "you are managing the dance perfectly."

Breathing a visible sigh of relief, she relaxed in his arms. "Thank goodness," she said with a twinkle to her eyes. "I would hate to botch up my first public attempt at it."

"You could never manage that. Not with me as your partner." He winked and twirled them both in a wide arc. "I simply wouldn't allow it."

"How gallant of you, my lord." She spoke with an exaggeratedly pompous note that immediately made him laugh.

Slowing their pace a bit, he quietly murmured, "Gallantry is one of my best qualities, Fiona." He deliberately waggled his eyebrows, which in turn made her laugh as well. Good. The gap that had formed between them these past few days was growing narrower. So he decided to aim for a bit of amicable conversation while they glided along among all the other couples. "The discovery Lamont and Laura made yesterday is interesting, don't you think?"

"Do you mean the letters or each other?"

A rumble of mirth rose up inside him. It shook

his shoulders. "Fiona!"

"What? It is a logical question considering the awkward position in which the two were discovered."

"And what would you know about that?" He really shouldn't be asking.

"Enough."

That was all she said, but it was sufficient to make his mind wander and his body react. *Christ*. He had to stay focused. So he cleared his throat. "I meant the letters, of course."

She blushed then – a deep and delightful hue that made him realize she'd only then become aware of how her previous statement might have sounded and to what it could have alluded. . "Yes. Naturally…" She drew a breath, expelled it again, and then paused for a second. "They obviously refer to the Cardinals."

"And they were written in exactly the same order as the ones we found carved into one of the stones in the passageway we went exploring that same afternoon."

She frowned in response to his statement. "What are you suggesting?"

"That maybe it was deliberate?"

She fell silent for a full rotation of the dance floor. Eventually she shook her head. "After what happened to Emily, I think it might be best if we stop searching for the treasure. No family heirloom or art collection is worth any of us dying over."

"I agree, although I do regret that it has to be like that." Tightening his hand against hers, he told her sincerely, "I know how much it meant for you to find those jewels."

"Not because of the worth." She looked away. "But it is all my family has left of my great-aunt and now, after discovering the sacrifices she made in order to help people, I really wanted her box to arrive at its designated destination, even if it were to arrive several decades later than intended."

Sympathizing with her, Edward drew her closer – so close their chests almost touched. He allowed his cheek to brush against hers in a daring way that was sure to elicit a few raised eyebrows and whispers from those who happened to see. But he didn't care. The only thing on his mind right now, besides offering comfort, was the sharp little gasp with which Fiona responded.

It made him want to do things – reckless things – things no young lady would even know were possible. Somehow he managed to hold himself in check while capturing the feel of her back against the palm of his hand, the sound of her breaths whispering past his ear. Inhaling deeply, he drew in her scent – wild citrus enriched with honey. He almost shuddered in response to the heady aroma. It coursed through his body, tightening each of his muscles until dancing with fluid movements became a cumbersome chore.

"Edward."

Unfortunately, she did not speak his name with breathless abandon or as though she longed for him to do all the things he dreamed of doing. With her. Together. Rather, her voice carried an admonishing note she'd only ever used before when she found him particularly annoying.

Drawing back, he looked her straight in the eyes. "Yes?"

"You're hurting my wrist."

Shifting, he glanced at his hand. Beneath him, his feet still managed to move in time to the rhythm by some miraculous force of habit drilled into him by the dance instructor he'd had as a child. It had always made it possible for him to think about anything he wished to besides the actual act of dancing without ever losing one step.

Until now, when he saw how hard his hand was clenching her.

He'd made the silk glove she wore twist and pucker beneath his white knuckles. Which resulted in the sole of his shoe coming down faster and harder than it was meant to as he hastily loosened his grip, and actually tripped. "Oh, Fee…" What explanation could he possible give? He'd behaved like a cad, allowing the fear of what could not be to affect a perfectly lovely dance. "Forgive me." He deliberately slowed his steps.

"Fee?" Her eyes grew large, as though everything else – the fact he'd caused her pain – meant nothing when compared to his unintentional slip of the tongue. "You've never called me that before," she pressed.

He shrugged as best as he could while trying to salvage what remained of their dance. "It's nothing – just the short form of your name."

"Of course." She frowned while focusing all her attention on some distant spot beyond his left shoulder.

He'd never felt like more of an ass. Except perhaps when he'd hurt her wrist while thinking the most lascivious things and then proceeding to stumble on top of it all. *Right*. He had to regain his composure.

The music finally faded — thank God — and he managed to execute a proper bow and then offer his arm without incident. *Good*. Things were returning to normal, except for the part where he wanted to throw her over his shoulder and run off to the nearest available bedroom. Or parlor. Really, at this point, any room with a horizontal surface would do. Except for the slight detail that she had no interest in that sort of thing. At least not with him. Which made him want to curse fate for making him want her so much he ached.

"I've often thought it," he said, drawing her toward the refreshment table.

She glanced at him with obvious surprise. "Thought what?"

"Of your name as Fee rather than Fiona." Her closed-off expression when he'd dismissed the endearment as 'nothing' had prompted him to explain. Even though he risked endangering his heart even more with this new confession. "It has a sprite-like connotation to it. I've always believed it suited your temperament."

CHAPTER TWENTY ONE

ACCEPTING THE GLASS OF CHAMPAGNE he placed in her hand, Fiona watched while he sipped his own, admiring how easily the rim of the glass fit against his full lower lip.

"What?" he asked, his gaze meeting hers when he lowered the glass once more.

Realizing she'd been caught staring, she gave a quick shrug of her shoulders and proceeded to drink some of her own bubbly liquid, enjoying the way it fizzed against her tongue. "I like Fee," she said, deliberately removing some of his attention from her and putting it right back onto the pet name he'd given her. When he'd first spoken it – as if it were the most natural thing in the world – she'd felt cherished in a way she'd never felt before. After all, none of her siblings had ever taken the time to give her a pet name, not that she'd ever felt as though she'd needed one. None of them had one really, except for Christopher, who'd always been called Kip.

But there was something wonderful about Chadwick giving her one. Because she loved him – yes, she might as well admit it to herself if not to anyone else – and the fact he'd thought about her enough to not call her what everyone else always called her. It made her feel special. More importantly, it made her feel as though she might matter to him a little bit more than she'd dared hope. Not that he'd ever feel half as much for her as she felt for him. She wasn't delusional after all. He'd made certain there would be no mistaking his affections when he'd spoken of maintaining their friendship and of how he considered her family – a sister, no doubt.

"Perhaps I should call you, Eddy, then?" She said it with a grin and with the hope of not getting all depressed while overthinking her platonic relationship with him. The truth was, she was fortunate to know him at all – fortunate to have him in her life – fortunate he cared enough about her to have paid as much attention as he had over the years.

"Do that and I may have to spank you."

She didn't miss the humor with which he spoke, but there was something else behind the words – something darker she couldn't quite seem to grasp. Oddly, it filled her brain with thoughts of kissing and other, far more scandalous things, like undressing – together. "You…" She found it impossible to speak all of a sudden.

His eyes widened, though not with the sort of awareness she was feeling but with concern. "Fiona." How she wished he would call her Fee again. "You do know I jest? I would never dream of actually hurting you like that."

Blinking, she allowed a nod. "Of course I do." Forcing a smile, she took another sip of her drink. A short distance away, the master of ceremonies raised his voice over the music and chatter, forcing the room into silence. It saved Fiona from having to continue the conversation at hand, which was just as well since she really did not know how to explain her startled response to his comment.

"Ladies and gentlemen." Lady Duncaster spoke once everyone had fixed their attention on the part of the room where she stood. "It is a delight to see you all here this evening, especially those of you who have travelled long distances. Thank you so much for coming." She paused for the right amount of time before adding, "As you know, Thorncliff has lent itself to romantic stirrings of the heart a few times already, and it seems it has done so again." A few hushed whispers circulated the room, tapering off when she spoke once more. "Lord and Lady Oakland. I am quite certain the guests are eager to hear your announcement."

Fiona waited for the announcement she knew was to come. She couldn't actually see anything, but then she heard her father's voice, loud and clear. "It is my greatest pleasure to inform you all here tonight that three of my daughters, Ladies Emily, Laura, and Rachel, are all engaged to be married. Though not to the same man, mind you." A bit of laughter rose in response. "Lady Emily will be marrying the Earl of Montsmouth; Lady Laura, the Duke of Lamont; and Lady Rachel will wed Viscount Belgrave. A toast, to all three couples!"

"Hurrah! Hurrah! Hurrah!" the crowd cheered. Fiona and Chadwick followed suit.

She was happy for her sisters – thrilled in fact. They had each found their happily ever after and would soon move on to enjoy fairy tales of their own making. "We should go and congratulate them."

She started forward but felt Chadwick's hand at her arm, holding her back. "Not until you've managed to regain your composure."

"What?"

He stepped around her, shielding her from everyone else and then leaned slightly in. His head dipped, moving closer until she could glimpse the fine creases that formed whenever he laughed. "You're crying, Fiona."

Raising her hand, she patted her cheeks. They were as damp as he'd suggested, which made no sense at all. She hadn't even realized she was doing it. "From joy," she assured him, because what other reason could there possibly be under the circumstances? The alternative would paint her as a selfish woman, unhappy her sisters were getting what she would not.

"Until your expression can convince them of that, I suggest you and I take that walk we discussed earlier." He linked his arm with hers and deliberately started leading her out through a side entrance.

"But—"

"We can borrow one of the throws from the green salon. No need for you to go all the way back upstairs for a shawl."

Unable to argue any further, she allowed her feet to fall into step with his. Somewhere deep inside her chest, little shards of what had to be the remains of her heart produced a stabbing effect that made her want to retreat. To keep his company now – alone – would be extremely difficult to endure.

And yet, some unknown part of her must have acquired a penchant for self-loathing, keeping her precisely where she was – as close to her source of pain as possible.

They reached the salon, and she allowed him to select a lovely wool throw in deep indigo. He set it about her shoulders before they stepped outside into the cool winter air. It wasn't as crisp as it had been a few days earlier, though she could still see her breath misting each time she exhaled.

"It's a beautiful evening," she said while he guided her across the wide expanse of terrace toward the steps beyond. This was where the masquerade ball had been held during the summer – where she and her sisters had sipped lemonade during the warm and breezy afternoons while watching croquet being played on the lawn below. It all seemed so long ago now. So much had happened, especially for them. Their lives had changed within only a couple of weeks.

"Will you tell me why your father's announcement was so upsetting to you?" Chadwick asked. "Do you even know?"

They headed down the steps that led toward the garden paths, several of which were now cleared of snow thanks to the two sunny days they'd had. As was to be expected at Thorncliff, they'd even been lined by lanterns, even though Fiona doubted anyone else would choose to leave the festive ballroom in favor of taking a chilly walk. She was glad she had though. Chadwick had been right. She'd needed a small reprieve, even though she hadn't known it herself.

"I don't," she lied.

Because really, how could she possibly tell him all she was feeling? How could she ever reveal her innermost thoughts – thoughts she hadn't yet shared with another soul?

She couldn't.

Not when those feelings involved him and stood to destroy whatever closeness they had. This private moment didn't offer as much as she wanted, but she would hold it close to her heart and cherish it with every fiber of her being if it was all there ever could be. To risk sacrificing it on a slim chance he might reciprocate…she almost laughed at her own fanciful stupidity.

He was eleven years older than she, after all. No doubt there existed some lady – an older and more sophisticated woman – who'd captured his heart. There was no reason for her to know about it. This was not the sort of thing gentlemen spoke of, least of all to a young girl barely out of the schoolroom.

"Could it be you wish for what they have?" His voice produced a gentle sound in the darkness.

It coaxed her to say, "It was a lot to take in all at once, even though I knew it was coming. I knew of my sisters' affections, but I never imagined things would move so quickly that I…" She swallowed the thought that flew to the surface and looked straight ahead. They were moving toward the lake.

"As you are the last remaining sister, I think it might have made you feel alone, perhaps even abandoned."

Her chest worked with her uneasy intakes of breath. The air was cool against her lungs, but the blanket offered a wonderfully warm cocoon that both soothed and offered comfort. Just as he did.

"Perhaps you're right. I have always been used to a house full of people, to laughter and noise, footsteps chasing each other up and down the stairs."

"That was always my favorite thing about your home," Chadwick said. They turned toward the left, following a path that would lead them toward the maze. "As well as you, of course, and your family."

"But all of that is going to change now, isn't it?" She considered how quiet it was going to be with no one else but her and her parents about. "To have three sisters move out all at once will make for quite a change."

"Until the day when you move out as well."

There was something in his voice, something almost regrettable that she couldn't quite figure out. So she made an effort to understand him. "You mean when I marry?"

"Naturally."

Now he sounded annoyed. She allowed the thought to sink in before shaking her head and telling him plainly, "I don't believe I will."

That stopped him in his tracks. He turned toward her, his face cast mostly in shadows save for a faint little sliver of silver that spilled from the moon to his brow. "Of course you will, Fiona. This feeling you're having right now…it will eventually pass. A new Season will begin, and you will meet a handsome and wonderful gentleman – someone kind who can make you laugh."

"Laughter is important," she said, because if she didn't speak she might burst into tears. "What other qualities will he have, do you think?"

Slowly, as if to ensure she was going to follow,

Chadwick resumed walking, speaking while he went. "If he doesn't own a large tree on his estate, then he must be willing to plant one so you will have something to climb."

She couldn't help but laugh. "I thought you told me I could no longer behave like a child."

"No." He fell silent for a moment before saying, "What I told you was that you and I have to *remember* you're no longer a child. There is a difference."

"I don't see—"

"There's no reason for you to stop having fun, Fiona, but for me to tickle you as I once did or give you a piggyback ride or anything else remotely like that would not be proper. Do you understand?"

"What I understand is that I'm to be miserable, Chadwick." She couldn't help herself from sharing that truth with him. "Playing and being silly with you – the tickling and the chasing and the…" She waved her arms about, searching for the right words. Failing, she had to settle for, "All of it." He'd gone completely quiet, no doubt from shock, but now she'd started she couldn't stop from adding, "I don't ever want to have to grow up if it means having to do without those things."

"In that case, we'll have to ensure the man you marry will be the sort to accommodate your playful nature."

She gave him a dubious look. "How likely do you suppose finding such an individual among our set is going to be?"

"Well, look at me. I'm like that."

"But you're not in the running. Are you?" The question was spoken without thinking. It simply flew from her mouth – a natural response to his comment. And now it was out there, floating between them, there was no taking it back. He'd heard her. His hesitance made that much perfectly clear. So she did the only thing she could think of in order to lessen the importance of what she'd said and the chance of him knowing how much it revealed. She laughed, pulled the blanket a little bit tighter, and used her most teasing tone. "Of course you're not. What a lark that would be."

He clamped his mouth on whatever he'd meant to say. Which was just as well since she really couldn't bear the thought of him telling her, "No." Or even worse, "Unfortunately, I'm planning to marry Lady Somethingorother instead."

They reached the entrance to the maze and paused there. The hedges weren't as dense as they'd been during the summer when leaves filled the gaps between the twining branches. "Do you wish to attempt it?" Chadwick asked.

She glanced up at him, hoping to read his expression. Unfortunately, there wasn't enough light for her to do so, so she considered his voice instead. It had sounded hopeful – perhaps because he knew as well as she did that this might be their last adventure together. In another few days they would both depart from Thorncliff. He would return to his own estate, and if the last four months were anything to go by, she might not see him again until they happened to meet at the same ball.

She closed her eyes for a second and took a deep breath. "Absolutely."

He grinned, even though his chest hurt. If only

she knew the severity of the blow she'd dealt with her hasty dismissal of him as a suitor. But she wouldn't consider him – her thoughts didn't even lie in that direction. No. He was nothing more than the good old family friend and brother figure with whom she enjoyed having fun. To suppose there was more than that on her part – that there ever could be – would be a mistake.

"Then by all means, my lady," he said, deliberately applying an affected tone he knew she'd find amusing, "allow me to escort you."

She made a chuckling sound, precisely as he'd expected, and placed her hand in the crook of his elbow. It felt so right he suddenly wished they might never find a way out of this maze – that by some poor chance of fate they might have to remain inside it forever. But they both knew the path inside out after giving the thing a thorough exploration the last time they'd visited, which meant it would take them roughly ten minutes to walk to the center and another ten to return. Twenty minutes was hardly forever, but it was going to have to make do since it was all he was being offered.

"I've been wondering," she said, after they'd gone a few paces. "Why haven't you married yet?"

His steps almost faltered, just as they had on the dance floor. "I don't suppose I had a reason to," he told her. There was some art to speaking the truth while carefully guarding one's emotions. "Why do you ask?"

"Curiosity." She curled her hand a bit more snuggly around his arm. "I know men don't have the same urgency to marry as women do, although you will eventually have to ensure there's an heir to your title."

"I'm only thirty years old, Fiona." Why did he need to remind her of that?

"Have you never met a woman – a lady, I mean – in all those thirty years with whom you might consider starting a family?"

Yes.

You.

How the hell was he supposed to be honest now? "Are you worried I might wait too long and eventually become one of those old doddering fools the young debutantes fear having to take to husband?"

Her shoulder nudged his as they rounded a corner, continued forward a few paces, and then turned right. "It is a justifiable concern."

"Then allow me to reassure you, I shall probably never marry." He hadn't meant to say that, but now the words were out, he realized how true they were. If he couldn't have Fiona…Christ, he'd have to sacrifice the title. It would end up going to his cousin's son, which wouldn't be too terrible since he rather liked that side of the family.

"Chadwick?"

He flinched at the realization that he must have missed part of the conversation. "Hmm?"

"What are you talking about?" Fiona asked.

She was no longer leaning into him but rather pulling back and looking up at him as if trying to gauge his expression. He doubted she could see more of his face in the darkness than he could of hers, for which he was glad. He didn't want her to notice how anxious he was.

"Well…" Oh, he'd done it now. He knew her well enough to know she would not be dropping this subject any time soon. "I have no wish to pick a random bride from a ballroom lineup and then proceed to court and marry her on the basis of her outstanding credentials. The prospect of it disagrees with me."

"Because of the man you are," Fiona said as though she knew him better than he knew himself. "You want more from a wife than for her to be simply a pedigree breeder."

Her frankness shouldn't have surprised him, and yet he still coughed in response to her statement. "Companionship might be nice as well," he managed to say.

"And love," Fiona quietly murmured in a way that made it clear this was one of her own requirements.

"Do you think it's possible to fall in love twice in a lifetime?" He'd no idea where that question had come from, yet somehow he'd spoken it anyway.

She hesitated before answering. When she finally spoke, her voice held a depth of honesty that made him wonder if he'd ever know the secrets of her heart. "I don't know."

"I think it is, but not without paying a price."

"How do you mean?"

"Well, I don't believe the two loves can ever be equal. One will always mean more than the other."

"And you think that would be unfair?"

"I do."

They continued in silence for a couple of minutes before she asked the question he had known she'd eventually ask. "Whom do you love, Chadwick?'

Her voice was small and fragile, so apart from her usual inquisitiveness. It was almost as if she feared the answer he might give her this time, which was likely his own mind playing tricks on him – a bit of wishful thinking that was sure to get him in trouble if he actually told her the truth.

"Does it matter?" he asked, instead. Turning left, the path opened up, revealing the large square center of the maze. Two benches stood here for those who wished to rest their feet before starting back, and there was a slender birch tree in one corner, offering partial shade during the summer.

"No," she whispered. "I don't suppose it does, though I cannot help but speculate."

Of course she couldn't. She'd always been curious, questioning everything and demanding answers. It made him wonder why they'd never had this conversation before. "There are some things I cannot discuss," he said. She slipped her arm from his and walked forward on her own. "Not even with you. I'm sorry." The throw was still wound tightly around her shoulders, producing a slim silhouette that looked awfully lonely standing there in the darkness. It prompted him to follow her, to offer comfort even though she'd said nothing to suggest this was what she needed.

And yet, he could sense something was wrong. Her mood was different than usual. She turned back to face him and took a sharp breath, no doubt startled by his sudden closeness. "I understand," she said. Two words that made it abundantly clear she did not understand anything at all, least of all the mangled state his heart was in.

"Fiona." He shook his head and gazed up. Perhaps the night sky would offer a solution. Instead, he found himself staring at the skeletal limbs of the birch tree, or more precisely at the thick cluster of leaves that hung like a ball from one of the nearest overhead branches. "Mistletoe."

"Where?"

"There," he said, pointing toward it. "We're standing right underneath it."

"Oh. I see."

He returned his gaze to hers, noting not only how close she was but that her chin was turned up at the exact right angle. *Kiss her.* He'd only have to lower his head, and she'd be right there waiting. His chest tightened like a knot. What a fool he'd be to pass up this opportunity – one that could easily be excused by the fortuitous presence of one little plant.

"Come on then," he said, forcing his most practical tone – as if he were only going to do what tradition compelled him to do. "It's supposed to be good luck."

He dipped his head, allowing her every opportunity in the world to retreat, to push him away or to tell him, "No." But she did none of those things. Instead, she remained where she was, waiting for him to do as he wished.

Slowly, so he could imprint every second of this experience to memory, he closed the distance, meeting her lips with his own in the softest, most perfect, caress he could ever have imagined. And it was as if time stood still and all that remained in the world was them – a perfect pair.

CHAPTER TWENTY TWO

IT WAS EVERYTHING SHE'D EVER dreamed of, and yet Fiona knew it couldn't possibly last. In another second or two, he would pull away and their kiss – the most precious kiss she would ever receive – would be over. So she did her best to focus on their point of contact – on what it felt like to have his lips pressed gently against hers. They were wonderfully soft and…

He drew back, forcing a sigh from somewhere deep down within. Except, she realized with startling awareness and even with her eyes still closed, that he hadn't gone far. She could feel his breath stirring her skin, the warmth of it pushing aside the cool winter air. And then his lips were suddenly on hers once more in a similar caress to the first one except this time, this time his hand found its way to the back of her head and held her steady – as if she might suddenly choose to run.

Confused and unsure of how to respond, she remained as still as a statue. Was it possible he actually *wanted* this? She could scarcely credit it. Not when she'd been so certain of his feelings. Except what should have been one brief and simple mistletoe kiss had now become two and… He shifted closer, his arm winding its way around her back in an intimate embrace and…and… Surely he wouldn't torment her like this unless he actually meant it. Would he? She had to know but was too afraid to ask, too afraid that the slightest sound might shatter the magic and make him remember she was Fiona, the girl he'd chosen to think of as Fee because it reminded him of a sprite. Not a goddess or siren or some other creature who might bring a man to his knees.

Still, she almost felt like a siren right now, for it did indeed feel as though he had trouble pulling away – of adding the expected distance that should have followed the first and especially the second chaste kiss. Instead, he pulled her closer, which was slightly awkward since her hands still clutched the throw tightly around her shoulders. He took another breath before covering her mouth with his once more, this time drawing her bottom lip between his in a way that carefully coaxed her open.

She heard him make a deep rumbling sound from somewhere inside his chest and could feel her heart respond with a rapid beat that echoed through every part of her body. Dear God, this had to be a dream of some sort. It couldn't possibly be real. And yet she felt him as keenly as she felt herself. His fingertips dug against her back, and his thumb scraped against her jaw while his mouth… oh yes, that glorious mouth was doing the most incredible things – so incredible she could feel the effect of it all the way to her toes.

He was like the rich champagne they'd enjoyed

in the ballroom, except better, and she wanted nothing more than to keep on drinking and tasting until she was thoroughly drunk on his flavor. Pushing her arms out from under the throw, she grasped at his shoulders, flattening her chest against his while he in turn deepened the kiss on a masculine groan that heated her blood. Evidently, he needed to taste her as much as she needed to taste him, and that wondrous thought made her want to both laugh and dance and hug him tight all at the same time.

Yes, it was real. Chadwick was actually kissing her now as though he was starving and she was a bountiful feast. His fingers were in her hair, his lips moving hungrily over hers as he licked his way forward, not only tasting her mouth but encouraging her to follow. And follow she did, pushing up close enough for her hips to make contact with his. She wanted to climb inside him and live there, if that made any sense at all.

"Fee." His voice was breathless when he broke off to trail a series of kisses along her cheek, and she couldn't help but smile with the knowledge that she had made him so. What a notion! "Christ, Fee…" He licked a moist path along the curve of her neck. "Please tell me you want this. Tell me this isn't a dream."

She grinned then, loving how stunned and befuddled he sounded. "It isn't a dream, Edward. You're kissing me and I'm kissing you. Because this is what I want more than anything else in the world."

"Oh God." The words came out raspy. He held her tight, his chest rising and falling so rapidly against her own, she feared he might suddenly burst. "Do you have any idea how much I've wanted…how I've longed…for this?"

"Hopefully, as much as I have," she whispered, a little surprised by the shyness she heard in her own voice. "I'm beginning to think we've both been quite foolish."

He pressed his forehead to hers while his hands worked to secure her throw more firmly around her shoulders, shielding her from the cold. "I was afraid you wouldn't reciprocate."

"So was I."

A light chuckle rumbled through him. "I see." His mouth found hers once again with more certainty this time, the scrape of his teeth against her lips producing a hot concoction of dizzying sensations somewhere deep in the pit of her belly. It prompted her to arch against him as though surrendering herself like a decadent offering most willing to be devoured.

"We should probably start back," he said, distancing himself a little. "If we don't…" She felt him shudder beneath her touch, as though he lacked control of his body.

"If we don't?" she prompted, not wanting the moment to end.

"I've wanted you for too damn long, Fiona, but I won't be a selfish cad out here in the freezing cold. You deserve better than that – we both do, truth is. But my restraint now that I know what you taste like is wearing dangerously thin. So I suggest we return to the ballroom and congratulate your sisters on their engagements."

"Oh. I see." She couldn't keep from smiling as

she loosened her hold on his jacket. "So then… what you're saying, if I understand you correctly, is if we were to stay here another minute or two, you'd have my skirts up around my waist on one of those benches while—"

"Fiona." His voice was dangerously low, the note of warning clear.

Giggling, she pushed her way past him and started making her way back as he had suggested while he followed behind. "You're lucky I'm in no mood to get sick, which I likely would if I were to bare myself to this unforgiving cold."

"Fiona." He sounded a bit more strangled now.

"Had we done this during the summer, however…well, that would have been an entirely different story."

"Bloody hell!"

"Can you imagine anything more perfect than making love beneath the stars?"

His arm swept around her waist, pulling her back so roughly she instinctively squeaked. The next thing she heard was his voice against her ear, his breath hot upon her skin while he whispered closely, "This isn't a game, Fiona. Have a care or I might not be able to stop myself from taking more than you ought to be willing to give me at this moment."

Stunned by his uncharacteristic gruffness and the elemental masculinity with which he spoke – as though he was tempted to toss her over his shoulder and carry her off to a cave for a wicked round of debauchery – she hesitated on the precipice where she now stood. He was right. They deserved better than a quick tumble on the frosty ground, which meant she would have to help him do the gentlemanly thing – the *right* thing for both of them.

"Promise me you will still want me tomorrow?"

He sighed against the back of her head. "It would be impossible for me not to, Fiona."

With that assurance, she blew out a breath of her own, her chest a little lighter and her hopes for the future a great deal brighter than they'd been half an hour earlier. "I still cannot believe this is real," she said as they stepped out from the maze and began following the path that would take them back to Thorncliff. "It seems like a dream."

"It isn't," he promised. Taking her hand, he set it upon his arm. "Now that I know you feel the same way, there'll be no going back. My feelings for you are as true as the North Star up there in the distance. See how it shines?"

"The North Star." She stared up at it for a moment. An idea began to emerge from the back of her mind. "Let's walk this way, Chadwick. I want to take a look at something." They continued until they'd reached a point that placed them halfway between Thorncliff's leftmost and rightmost wall. Stopping there, Fiona looked back at the grand estate and smiled. "It's a compass, Chadwick. I cannot believe I didn't think of it before."

"Good lord. You're right!"

"And with the Cardinals taken into account – their choice of code names being the North, South, East and West Wind…" She fell silent, dumbfounded by her own ignorance. "I think the most important clue to the treasure has been staring us in the face all along."

"The wind rose inlay in the foyer floor?"

Nodding, she glanced up at him. "Not once did I look at it as anything other than a pretty design, but I'm beginning to think there has to be more to it than that."

"It is supposed to indicate the direction from which the wind blows on a map." Tugging her arm, he began leading her back up toward the terrace. "In any case, you will have to wait for the guests to leave before going ahead with this new part of your investigation."

"I told you earlier, I have no intention of continuing after what happened to Emily."

A snort was his immediate response, and then he said, "I know you did, but this is the sort of breakthrough that's going to nag at you until you agree to take a closer look at it. Just as long as you let me help you and promise me you'll be careful."

"Of course." She could scarcely contain the excitement that bubbled inside her. It made her want to race up the steps to the terrace and hurry toward the foyer. Instead, she forced herself to maintain a more ladylike stride. Her sisters required her attention first, as did the ball, while the wind rose would easily wait for another few hours, even if her fingers were itching to explore it with immediate haste.

CHAPTER TWENTY THREE

"I CANNOT BELIEVE YOU ARE ALL to be married," Fiona said. Those who'd simply come to attend the ball had departed half an hour earlier, leaving the Heartlys, Lamont, Belgrave, Montsmouth, Edward, and Lady Duncaster to enjoy a bit of tea before retiring.

"Neither can we," Lady Oakland exclaimed with a loving smile directed at her husband. "But it is marvelous. We really couldn't be happier."

"You will be sure to make headlines," Lady Duncaster said. Her eyes caught Edward's for a second as though in thoughtful contemplation. He found himself holding his breath until she looked toward Lord and Lady Oakland once more. "It is no small feat to marry off six children in the space of one year."

"The gossip rags will have a marvelous time of it," Laura remarked. "Perhaps we should stop by the Mayfair Chronicle after departing from here and set our story straight – allow one of the journalists there to interview us before any suppositions are made."

"I think that's an excellent suggestion," Lord

Oakland said. "By then we might even be able to give them a proper account of the weddings."

"I was actually hoping to visit the paper before the weddings, Papa." Laura reached for Lamont's hand and gave it a gentle squeeze – a gesture Edward wished he could replicate with Fiona. But he'd yet to make his intentions known, not only to her family but to her.

With her sisters' engagements in mind and Fiona's new realizations regarding the treasure, he hadn't yet managed a proposal of his own. Which was maybe for the best since their history together made him want to do something particularly special – something worthy of her.

"If we have to wait three weeks or more," Laura continued, "the news or some version of it will already have reached London. What I would like to suggest is for us to —"

"Marry here," Lord Oakland said with a grin he apparently shared with not only his wife but with Lady Duncaster too. "What can possibly be more romantic than a three-fold Christmas wedding?"

"But…" It was Rachel's turn to speak. "Christmas is in only two days. That's not nearly enough time for the banns to be cried."

A moment of silence passed. The Oaklands and Lady Duncaster all looked like three conspiratorial children who'd gotten caught in the middle of a prank. Sensing the next words spoken were going to be extremely interesting indeed, Edward leaned forward in his seat and eyed Fiona, who appeared to be as intrigued as he felt.

"The truth is," Lady Oakland began, "that we – your father and I, that is – came to Thorncliff prepared for this eventuality."

Lord Oakland considered each of his daughters in turn. "What your mother is trying to say is, we had the foresight to procure special licenses for all of you, in case you wished to have a Christmas wedding."

"But…" Emily frowned. "You couldn't have known Montsmouth and I would fall in love or that he would propose or that Rachel would end up with Belgrave and Laura with Lamont. Each couple's name would have to be on each license, paired off in a way not even you could have predicted."

Lord Oakland raised an eyebrow. "Perhaps not, but Lady Duncaster did."

Everyone turned to regard their hostess, who met their inquisitive stares with a brilliant smile. Shrugging, she reached for her tea and took a sip. "I spent a great deal of time observing all of you when you were last here during the summer. I noted your interests and your personalities and used that information to determine how to make the most appropriate matches. All that was needed after that was the opportunity for you to become better acquainted with each other. Coming here for Christmas seemed like an excellent plan – especially since Lord and Lady Oakland were more than thrilled by the idea of seeing the rest of their children settled."

"So this has been a matchmaking party all along?" Belgrave asked.

"In a manner of speaking," Lady Duncaster confirmed. "You can't be too surprised, what with four bachelors and four unattached ladies being brought together under the same roof."

Lamont ran his hands through his hair. "Well, I'll be…"

"Of course, it has also been a wonderful diversion for me," Lady Duncaster added. "I have no family with whom to celebrate the holiday season otherwise." She eyed Lamont. "Your company in recent years has been greatly appreciated, but I craved the boisterousness of a larger group." Glancing at everyone else in turn, she told them sincerely, "Spending time with all of you – filling the house with chatter and laughter – has been a treat."

"So if I am to understand you correctly," Rachel said in her typically concise manner that spoke of a need to make sense of the world, "we can marry as soon as we wish?"

"Correct," Lord Oakland said.

"The chapel is at your disposal," Lady Duncaster said. "Unless, of course, you desire a large London wedding and more time to order new gowns and so forth, in which case you will have to wait."

"I have no need of a new gown," Laura said. "In my opinion a Christmas wedding sounds delightful."

"I couldn't agree more," Lamont told her with a smile.

The other two couples concurred, and it was quickly decided the chapel should be decorated with pine garlands, ribbons, and candles. Edward had no doubt it would provide a romantic setting for a wedding, not to mention there was something particularly special about getting married on Christmas.

He glanced at Fiona, whose attention appeared

to be drawn by her mother at the moment. Not once did she look across at him, no matter how much he willed her to do so, and he couldn't help but wonder at what she might be thinking. Was she disappointed her sisters were getting married so quickly while she was not? Did she feel excluded? He could easily rectify that with a quick question, except he didn't want to rush a proposal. It would be the only one he would ever make, so he wanted to get it right.

He would wait for just the right moment. One that would hopefully present itself soon enough to allow Fiona the chance to marry on Christmas as her sisters were now quite eagerly planning to do. He couldn't help but grin at their animated faces as the women spoke of the shopping they'd have to do tomorrow at the village, while each of the soon to be bridegrooms stared at them in bemusement. It was already three o'clock in the morning, yet none of those present – not even Lady Duncaster – seemed remotely tired. He rose with the intention of excusing himself and heading off to bed. If he was going to plan the perfect proposal, he would have to do so on more than a few hours of sleep.

Except Fiona stood as well, blocking his path to the door. "Before you go…" What? Was she going to propose to him? That would certainly make his task a lot easier. She twisted so she could address the whole group. "I planned to give up on finding the treasure after Emily's terrible mishap."

Ah yes, the treasure.

"That passageway has been closed off since then," Lady Ducaster assured everyone. "I have also asked for access to be denied to the rest of the tunnels until they can be properly mapped. The last thing we need is for one of my guests to get lost down there for good. It's simply too dangerous."

"I agree," Fiona said, "but there is still the question of the wind rose in the foyer."

"The wind rose?" Lady Duncaster stared at Fiona for a long moment with parted lips and then sank back against her seat with a great big sigh. "Of course!"

"What are you talking about?" Emily asked.

Fiona explained. "Historically, wind roses have been placed on maps in order to show the direction the major winds are blowing. It therefore stands to reason that the one in the foyer might be linked to the Cardinals – the North, South, East and West winds, as they called themselves."

"Especially since that floor was put in by my father-in-law years ago when he remained here to oversee some renovations while my husband and I were in London," Lady Duncaster said. "I don't know why I never considered its significance before."

"I suppose we were all looking for a secret room and finding one in the foyer seemed unlikely, but after following the tunnels underneath, Chadwick and I determined they all stopped or turned in some way when they reached the vicinity of the foyer. We were never able to pass directly underneath, leading me to believe something might be there – some hidden space we've yet to find the entrance to."

"I suppose we ought to go and look at the foyer then," Rachel said.

"My thoughts exactly," Fiona agreed. She was

already heading for the door.

Edward followed close behind, intent on sharing each moment of her discovery. He'd find time to think about his proposal later. But when he arrived in the foyer, he had to wonder if Fiona's hypothesis could be true since it seemed impossible for any man to have manufactured something as extraordinary as what Fiona was suggesting, and during the course of only one year and without any servant being the wiser.

Still, he watched with interest while Fiona marched into the center of the wind rose and glanced around the room. Her hands were on her hips, offering her a look of decisive determination. "N.E.W.S," she said. That is what you found on your way to the study, is it not?"

Laura, who'd turned a fetching shade of pink, nodded. "It is."

"Right, then." Fiona walked in the direction the northern point of the wind rose indicated, and Edward realized it didn't lead her straight toward the front door like he'd initially imagined it would.

The thing was slightly off center – a fact he'd never noticed before. But he did so now while he watched Fiona reach the wall. A painting hung there, and she proceeded to run her fingers across it, then along the outside edges of the frame until she suddenly paused. She seemed to push forward on something – a button or lever perhaps – and Edward heard a distinct click.

Fiona spun around, facing them all with a grin. "I think I've figured it out!"

She hurried across the floor, following the eastern point of the wind rose to where another painting hung. There, she found a similar spot on which to push down and produce a clicking sound. The western point came next followed by the southern. Here, Fiona paused. Edward went to where she stood and placed his hand on her shoulder. "Go ahead. Let's see what happens next."

"I could be wrong," she whispered.

"Yes. You could be. But you won't know unless you try."

She pushed down below the painting, and he could see now that it was a small lip protruding from the wall. It almost looked as though it had been placed there to help anchor the painting, unless one studied it closely enough to see that the painting didn't touch it at all. A second of silence followed, and then Edward heard a distinct whirring sound.

"Stand back," he told everyone while he and Fiona stared down at the floor before them. The wind rose was sinking and turning, the inlaid pieces of marble twisting outward and disappearing into the sides of what turned out to be a large spiral staircase.

"Oh my God," Fiona murmured, then caught herself and slapped her hand over her mouth.

"I think it's all right for you to say that, under the circumstances, Fiona," Edward muttered. He glanced across at the rest of the group. Each person was staring at the newly revealed staircase with shock and awe. Lady Duncaster herself appeared as though she might stumble and fall. Thankfully, Lord Oakland was quickly beside her, offering her his assistance.

"Is that really there?" she asked, pointing one finger toward the first steps leading downward. "Am I actually seeing that?"

Assurances were made while Edward, Belgrave, Lamont, and Montsmouth went to fetch lanterns. "I'll go first," Edward said when he returned. "Fiona, you may follow directly behind me, if you wish." She frowned at him but didn't argue, for which he was grateful. After all, they were about to explore a place that had been sealed off for decades, so he wasn't about to take any chances with Fiona going first, no matter how much she probably wanted to do so.

Still, he occasionally felt her hand at his waist as they made their descent, the lantern casting an intimate glow against the solid stone walls while they went. Behind him, he could hear the chatter of those who'd chosen to join him and Fiona on this new little adventure, their voices reverberating in a ghostly way that made it impossible for him to determine their closeness. He counted thirty steps before arriving on a solid dirt floor. Turning up the flame of the lantern, he stepped out from behind a pillar in the center of the staircase and studied the space beyond, almost catching his breath at the sight he beheld. "Incredible."

"This is it," Fiona whispered, stepping up beside him. She hesitated there for a second before continuing forward, her feet seemingly drawn to the wondrous collection of carefully wrapped items and boxes, all grouped in various clusters with each containing a label informing the viewer of where the pieces had come from. "Look here. This is from the Gavrois family. And these over here, they have come from the Comte D'Orly." It was a staggering display of artifacts, no doubt about that. "Look, Edward!"

His heart expanded in response to Fiona's use of his name. He glanced around, wondering if anyone else had noticed, but they all seemed to be too preoccupied themselves. So he went to where she was standing and placed his hand at her elbow. "What is it?"

Her fingers traced a label attached to a large trunk. *Le Duc et La Duchesse de Marveille.* "These items here belonged to my great-aunt." She gave Edward a brief glance – enough for him to see the sheen of moisture that covered her eyes. "I'm almost afraid to look."

"Do you want me to do it?"

Snatching her fingers back, she stepped aside and nodded, allowing Edward to undo the latch. Carefully, he eased the lid back, revealing the contents. A piece of black velvet fabric was the first thing that came into view. It had been laid out, covering the rest of the items, as if to offer some sort of protection. Edward lifted one end and folded it to the side, then paused as his gaze fell on the items it had been hiding. There were a few books, a couple of decorative porcelain pieces, a clock, but most importantly, a wooden box carved with the scene of a shepherdess tending her sheep. He lifted it out and held it toward Fiona. "I think this is what you've been looking for."

Her lip trembled, and she hesitantly placed her hand upon the lid. "You found it." She swallowed, then took a deep breath and slowly pushed the lid open. Edward couldn't help but stare at the dazzling selection of gemstones that came into view.

"Oh my goodness." He looked up to see tears had spilled from Fiona's eyes and immediately felt his heart clench in response. "There's the tiara she received from the Empress of Russia. Oh…it's so beautiful, all of it, don't you think?"

Reaching up, Edward brushed his thumb across her cheek, wiping away the tears. "It is an extraordinary find," he whispered.

"I have to show Mama and Papa." Smiling, she turned to do precisely that when Lady Oakland called to them from the other side of the room.

"You must come and see this, all of you," the countess said in an eager tone that raised Edward's curiosity. He followed Fiona over to where her mother was leafing through some papers that had been strewn about on a table. "I found these in that portmanteau over there." She gestured toward the discarded leather satchel with a wave of her hand.

"What is it?" Rachel asked as she, Emily, and Laura drew closer together with their fiancés. Lord Oakland and Lady Duncaster stepped up alongside them until everyone surrounded the countess.

"Birth certificates – twenty of them, to be exact. And there's a letter as well." Lady Oakland bowed her head over the piece of paper she was holding. "It reads as follows: 'There is a chance my comrades and I will all be long gone before these treasures are found. That has always been our intention since time alone would serve to preserve our most important secret and keep the people who trust us safe. We have done what we could, even though we wish we could have done more. Too many innocents perished during the Terror, but at least we were able to save a few. These children were brought to England under the cover of night, ensuring their families would find continuation by blood, if not by title. They have been placed in modest homes, safely hidden from the Electors and anyone else who may wish to harm them. Experience has taught me that few people in this world can be trusted, which is why no clues will be left to their whereabouts. Hopefully, this will prevent those who wish to undo our work from meeting with any success while assuring our descendants we did what could be done in the name of both life and freedom. Signed, Robert Everton Hayworth, the 3rd Earl of Duncaster.'"

Silence remained for seconds after until Lady Duncaster finally spoke. "I think I need a brandy now."

"I believe I'll join you," Lord Oakland said. He started escorting her back upstairs.

"I can scarcely believe it," Laura murmured. "This is truly more incredible than anything I ever thought we might find."

"And there is this as well," Fiona said. She stepped forward and placed the jewelry box on the table.

"Oh, my dear," her mother exclaimed. "You actually found it!"

"There will be a lot of work to do, cataloguing all of the items here," Montsmouth said. "I must confess it far exceeds my expectations."

They returned upstairs moments later with the intention of taking a closer look at their discovery over the course of the next few days. It was even decided they would make an effort to return whatever was possible for them to return to any surviving members of the families who'd placed their valuables in Duncaster's safekeeping. In the meantime, the party would disperse to their individual bedrooms for some much needed rest.

Edward escorted Fiona to the top of the stairs and paused there to wish her good night. "Perhaps we can go for a ride tomorrow, if the weather permits?"

She was clutching the jewelry box as if she feared it might suddenly vanish. "Yes. I would like that."

Instinct tempted him to dip his head and kiss her, but her sisters and parents were passing right behind her on the way to their own bedchambers, so he resisted the urge. "Good night then," he murmured instead, waiting until she had moved out of sight before turning toward the left and heading in the direction of his own room.

CHAPTER TWENTY FOUR

WHEN FIONA WOKE LATE THE following morning, she lay for a long while staring up at the ceiling. It almost seemed as though the previous evening had never happened. Chadwick…Edward…had actually kissed her beneath the stars and with so much passion she was surprised she hadn't melted on the spot. And they'd found the treasure – a collection of items so impressive, she could scarcely credit its existence. Oh, and her sisters were going to get married tomorrow in the small chapel where Kip had spoken his vows to Sarah.

Sighing with the pleasure of it all, she stretched out her arms before letting herself relax into a collection of languid limbs. This visit to Thorncliff had certainly met with success from a number of different angles. Recalling Edward's suggestion the previous evening that they go for a ride today, she flung the coverlet aside and got up, ignoring the chill that seeped into her feet from the cool floor underneath. A fire would be stoked by a maid, as soon as she called for one to assist. She did so presently, and ten minutes later she was able to warm herself and her toes in front of the fireplace while changing out of her nightdress and pulling on her chemise, stays, and gown. She'd selected a deep blue velvet today since she knew blue was Edward's favorite color.

Hurrying from her bedchamber, she half walked, half skipped in her excitement to get downstairs and speak with her family about the treasure and spend more time with Edward. He hadn't mentioned his intentions last night, but she knew he wouldn't kiss her like that and then simply go on as if nothing had happened. He would have things to say – things she was more than ready to hear.

She rounded a corner, her feet skidding slightly in her haste to reach the dining room, and immediately collided with a solid surface. "Oomph!"

"Fiona." Edward's eyes danced with amusement even as his voice held a note of concern. "Are you all right?"

He'd caught her by the shoulder, his hand still resting there now, and she felt that bit of contact so keenly, it was as if a fire had been struck against her skin. "Yes." Heavens, she sounded breathless.

Grinning down at her, he removed his hand and stepped back a little. "I don't suppose I might be the cause of your eagerness this morning?"

She immediately felt herself blush. "And what if you are? Would that please you?"

His eyes seemed to darken a fraction, and she suddenly felt a little unbalanced. They were flirting with each other – an entirely new scenario with which she wasn't familiar. "Indeed," he murmured in a low tone that made her insides ripple with awareness. "It would please me a great deal."

Her heart pitter-pattered like an anxious little rabbit, and yet all she wished to do was fling her arms around him and pull him close. She wanted to return to what they'd had last night with a desperation that made her feel utterly reckless. "Then… er…" Good Lord, she couldn't think of what to say next, which was most unusual.

"Eat your breakfast and meet me by the front door in half an hour," he told her seriously. "I'm going to prepare our carriage."

With this glorious thought in mind, Fiona headed off to endure the longest half hour of her life. But it turned out to be well worth the wait as soon as she saw what he had prepared. "This is quite wonderful," she said, once he'd handed her up into the carriage and taken the seat beside her. Thick fur pelts had been laid out on the seats, while a heater with hot coals in it sat at their feet offering warmth.

"I'm glad you think so," Edward said, spreading a thick wool blanket across both of their laps. He slid a bit closer, and she felt his thigh against hers, the scandalous contact blazing a trail along her entire left side. He didn't seem to notice as he tapped on the roof and the carriage jerked into motion.

Fiona held her breath. She was scarcely able to think, let alone move for fear the slightest action on her part might prompt Edward to add a proper measure of distance. "I like the blue," he murmured close to her ear.

"I imagined you would. It is, after all, your favorite color."

He chuckled lightly. "This is the wonderful thing about us, Fiona. We know each other so well that being together like this, in a new kind of way, adds a depth to the experience I think most couples lack." His hand found hers beneath the blanket, pulling it out so he could place a kiss upon her knuckles. "No gloves?"

"I didn't want them between us." She could tell by the slight widening of his eyes he hadn't expected her to be quite so honest, but she was glad she'd had the courage. It would make things simpler for both of them in the end.

"There will never be anything between us, ever again, Fee."

She drew a sharp breath, and his mouth descended once more, this time upon her own. His lips were as warm and soft as they'd been the evening before, but the taste of champagne had since disappeared, replaced by the smooth aroma of coffee. She turned more fully toward him, her hands rising to hold him close by the nape of his neck and the back of his head, her fingers reveling in the silky caress of his hair. A growl rose from somewhere deep within his chest, and she instinctively caught it with her mouth, loving the way it hummed through her body. His arms reached around her, and he leaned in, pushing her back against the corner of the squabs, his mouth hard against hers while he gave and took in equal measure.

"Fiona." Her name was spoken like a breathless benediction, the word stroking at the edge of her soul and leaving her desperate for more. He leaned in, pressing closer, so close she could feel the strength and vitality rippling through him, the hard planes of his body in a snug embrace with her much softer curves.

"Yes?" she whispered while he kissed his way along the curve of her neck.

"I want you so much it hurts," he confessed before playfully scraping his teeth against her flesh in a way that sent sparks of pleasure spiraling through her. "Forgive me, Fiona…Christ, I'm making a hash of this."

"Of what?" She could scarcely speak.

He buried his face against the curve of her neck, his breaths coming fast and ragged, like he was struggling to regain control. Eventually he drew back, and the expression on his face made it clear he did so with great difficulty.

"I love you, Fiona. I've loved you for quite some time now." He blurted the words as though fearing he might lose his nerve. It afforded him with a degree of hesitance that went straight to her heart. "I love you with a soul-wrenching desperation that makes me feel mad most of the time. The desire to be with you, to share every fine detail of my life with you, is so acute it makes me tremble to think you might not feel the same. But the way you returned my kiss last night and now makes me dare to ask the most important question of all: if you will have me, my heart, my love. Marry me, Fiona, and—"

"Yes!"

"Yes?"

"Most assuredly, yes." Her arms wrapped tightly around his shoulders, her fingers reaching for his hair, tunneling through it in an almost crazed determination to touch every part of this man who'd come to mean so much. "I love you too, Edward." She whispered the words and drew in his scent – that familiar blend of sandalwood, musk, and coffee that made her feel safe, comforted, cared for.

He blew out a shuddering breath and returned his lips to the side of her neck, kissing her there until she sighed and arched, wishing they were already married and anywhere other than in an impractical carriage. He must have felt the same, for his arms shook with self-imposed restraint while he held her and quietly said, "Let us hope your parents had the foresight to procure a special license for us as well. Because honestly, I cannot imagine having to wait three weeks in order to make you mine. As long as you agree, of course."

She pulled him back for a kiss, telling him without words that her need for him was equal to his need for her. Even a day seemed like an insufferable amount of time to wait. Which was why she asked that they cut their ride short and return to Thorncliff immediately. "I want to inform Mama and Papa right away and ensure that marrying tomorrow is indeed a possibility."

Edward didn't argue. He even held her hand the entire way back and was still holding firmly onto it when they burst through the door to the green parlor where the rest of their party was gathered. All conversation ceased, and everyone turned to acknowledge their abrupt arrival. Fiona felt her cheeks flush as she tried to calm herself – her breaths had quickened when she'd leapt from the carriage and half walked, half run the necessary distance.

"You look as though you blew in on a gust of wind," Lady Duncaster remarked from her position in one corner.

"I…We…" Fiona stared at her family's expectant faces.

Fiona's mother raised her eyebrows. "Yes?"

"I have asked Fiona for her hand in marriage," Edward said, his hand tightening around hers with the sort of masculine possessiveness that made her feel incredibly cherished. "And she has accepted."

A momentary hush fell over the room, and then Lord Oakland was suddenly on his feet and striding toward them. "About bloody time," he declared with a grin and then immediately apologized for his language. He stuck out his hand to Edward who gave it a firm shake, the relief he felt coming off him in waves.

Fiona hadn't realized until that moment how nervous he'd been about telling her parents, which was silly, of course. She'd had no doubt in her mind they would be pleased to make him a more permanent part of the family.

"It took you long enough." Laura grinned. She came to give Fiona a hug. "If I'd had to place a bet, I would have said with confidence that the two of you would become engaged long before any of us."

"I couldn't agree with you more," Emily said.

Rachel nodded. "Considering how close you have always been, marriage did seem like the next logical step."

"You are aware, my dear," Belgrave said to Rachel, "that the heart cannot be dictated by logic. Though I must confess that where you and Fiona are concerned, Chadwick, we were all surprised by how long it took you to get to the point."

"The important thing is, he got there in the end,"

Lamont said as he too came to shake Edward's hand.

"Felicitations to you both," Montsmouth said, "and to you, Lord and Lady Oakland. You may now consider all of your children settled."

"I trust you will want to say your vows tomorrow as well?" Fiona's mother asked with a smile.

"If doing so is possible." It was difficult for Fiona to hide her eagerness.

Her father chuckled. "Of course it is. In fact, your special license was the only one I had no doubts about procuring, which made it all the more surprising when your sisters announced their engagements first."

"I'm sorry, Papa," Fiona said. She smiled up at Edward who met her gaze with enough love and affection shining in his eyes to last her a lifetime. "We were both stubborn, I suppose, and too afraid of what the other might feel. I didn't want to risk our friendship, and neither did he. Thankfully, the universe had different plans for us, and a bit of conveniently located mistletoe nudged us in the right direction."

"Thorncliff does have a tendency to help things along like that," Lady Duncaster said, a twinkle in her eyes. "Personally, I have to tell you all that I couldn't be more pleased with the way everything has turned out. I do so love a good romance, and as I've said before, I believe everyone deserves a happily ever after."

Fiona couldn't agree more. She'd certainly found hers. And as she spoke her vows the following day, surrounded by the people she loved most in all the world – save for Kip, Chloe, and Richard, who would likely expire from shock when news of the quadruple wedding reached them – she'd never been happier.

Dressed in a pretty lace gown and with her great-aunt's tiara adorning her hair, Fiona felt a comforting connection to a generation that was no longer with them. If only her grandmother could have seen her four granddaughters now, each carrying a piece of Marveille jewelry when they entered a new phase in their lives. The sentimental thought brought a tear to her eye while bright rays of sunshine illuminated the stained glass windows at that exact moment.

"Merry Christmas," Edward murmured. He dipped his head with the clear intention of sealing their union with a kiss.

"Merry Christmas," she whispered back, right before his lips touched hers. She was vaguely aware of her parents and Lady Duncaster cheering, along with Lamont's nieces and the servants, who'd been invited to witness the joyous event. They would walk back to Thorncliff together through the soft sprinkling of new-fallen snow. There they would enjoy a wedding breakfast, followed by games and the exchanging of gifts. It would likely take several hours before Fiona would manage to get her husband alone, not that she minded terribly much. The important thing was, they'd gotten this far and that they were as fortunate as they were to be surrounded by love for Christmas.

CHAPTER TWENTY FIVE

WHEN FIONA FINALLY MADE HER way up the grand staircase that evening, her stomach was so unsettled she feared she might be violently ill. Ahead of her, her sisters whispered and giggled with their husbands before calling a hasty, "good night" to her and Edward as they disappeared toward whichever room they had planned to occupy that night. All appeared self-assured and eager, while Fiona felt a mixture of excitement and dread. This was going to be the most important night of her life, and she didn't want to muck it up. On the contrary, she wanted it to be everything Edward hoped it would be. In short, she wanted him to be pleased and satisfied with his decision to make her his wife.

"I think you need to relax," he said when they reached the landing and turned left.

"I am relaxed."

Her lie was met with a chuckle. "Whatever concerns are occupying that pretty head of yours, I do wish you'd put them to rest."

She had no chance to respond before her feet were swept out from underneath her, and she was being lifted up into the air only to find herself suddenly – and rather awkwardly – flung across his shoulder as he marched along the hallway. "Edward!" Her outraged remark was punctuated by an unwilling squeal of laughter when he gave her backside a solid slap.

"I told you I might have to set you across my knees for a spanking."

"Put me down!" She tried to kick her legs, which proved difficult since they were being restrained by an incredibly strong arm. *Good heavens!* When on earth had Edward managed to become so fit? Or maybe he'd always been so, and she hadn't noticed because she'd been seeing him in a different, more brotherly, light?

Well, that was no longer the case. She was now acutely aware of the wide shoulder on which her belly rested and the fact he carried her as though she weighed nothing at all.

"Just a moment," she heard him say with a touch of humor infusing his voice. He paused to open a door, then continued on through to a room, kicking the door shut with the heel of his shoe, while her head dangled against his back and her arms did what they could to punch at his sides.

"Stop it, you willful little hoyden." He spun around, making her squeal once more. Good lord, whatever would the rest of the household think they were up to? She wriggled her bottom, and he muttered something beneath his breath before she felt his hands on her waist. They lifted her down and planted her unceremoniously on the floor.

She stared at his bright expression, at his animated eyes, those lips that curved with unmistakable mischief, dimpling on either side. It brought out her own playful nature while emboldening her with the memory of what it had always been like between them. Why couldn't it remain that way once they were married? She had no answer for that, so she chose instead to take a step back, edging her way around the bed and offering him the most teasing look she could manage. "You're obviously up to no good as usual," she declared. Her fingers trailed along the nearest bedpost.

He took a step forward, and she retreated once more. "Will you reprimand me?" His hands went to his neck, unfastening his cravat while her eyes followed the movement with fascinated curiosity.

"Should I?" She'd no idea what she was saying or why, but the words seemed to add a curious sense of urgent expectation to the overall mood of the room. Her mouth went dry when he shrugged out of his jacket and tossed his cravat aside.

His eyes studied her with a wolfish gleam she recognized from when he'd straddled her in the forest and kissed her in the maze. It heated her skin and melted her insides, producing a gooey mess only he would be able to put to right once more.

"I think not," he murmured, still moving toward her. She'd reached the other side of the bed, her eyes hastily taking in the massive size of the mattress. He followed her gaze and smiled. "On the contrary, I think it is I who should reprimand you."

"On what grounds?" Was that really her voice? It had never sounded so sultry before.

"On account of the fact that you take no pity in stripping me of my senses." He lunged for her, but she quickly avoided his grasp, laughing with unabashed glee as she leapt onto the bed and bounced to the opposite side. He flung himself after her, forcing a shriek from her when he caught her around the waist and sent her toppling. "Got you!"

She landed with him on top, his hands caging her as he held her in place with his body. Her breaths faltered and awareness set in – his hard planes pressing her into the soft mattress, his legs snug against hers while he braced himself on his elbows and gazed down at her upturned face.

Swallowing, he shifted his gaze to her lips, and the grin he'd been wearing instantly faded. And then he was suddenly kissing her, his mouth chasing hers with a hunger she'd never believed possible, while his hands – the same hands that had helped her down from the stable roof once and tickled her senseless whenever they'd played – were seemingly everywhere. They stroked along her thigh, grabbed at her waist, pressed against her breasts and wound their way through her hair, while tugging and tearing her clothes from her body with a swift efficiency that left her marveling at his skill.

"God help me, I cannot wait." He pulled off his own clothes and settled himself between her thighs.

"Then don't." Her eyes met his, and she arched up against him – a natural instinct that brought him closer – inviting him to join his body with hers in the most elemental way possible. And so he did, his nimble fingers easing the otherwise painful transition and filling her body with light and warmth and an ever-increasing need for more.

"Fiona." Her name was wrenched from him on a growl of wanton pleasure when he rocked his hips forward, teaching her the movements that would send them both soaring. And soar they did, while kisses rained down on both their faces and fingers splayed across their heated flesh. It brought a sensory satisfaction so intense, Fiona was certain she saw stars spark behind her eyes as she fell apart in his arms.

"I love you," he whispered against her ear.

"As I love you," she promised, clinging to him for support while he carried her through their passionate storm.

For long moments after, she felt as though she was drifting in a languorous, dreamlike state. Then his arm wound around her, catching her weightless limbs in a tight embrace that secured her to his side. His lips grazed her temple, and he curled himself around her, molding their bodies together beneath the thick duvet.

Peering through the darkness at the leaded glass window, Fiona saw that snow was falling once more. A beam of moonlight illuminated the tiny flakes that fell to the ground like blossoms spilling from fruit trees. The effect was made all the more magical with the sound of wood crackling in the fireplace and the feel of her husband hugging her tight. "This has, without a doubt, been the best day of my life," she whispered.

His lips found her shoulder in a tender caress. "Merry Christmas," he murmured as he swept her away on another wave of pleasure.

EPILOGUE

"CAN YOU BELIEVE IT'S ALREADY been a year since our wedding?" Fiona asked Edward when he handed her a glass of mulled wine. The scent of cinnamon rose from the hot liquid as she set the rim to her lips for a careful sip.

Bowing, he leaned in, as close as he possibly could. "Happy anniversary, my love," he whispered, producing a lovely rush of heat all over her body. He must have said it a dozen times throughout the day – first, when he'd kissed her awake that morning while dangling a brilliant amethyst pendant before her sleepy eyes.

"I told you they'd make a perfect match," Richard said from his position on a nearby sofa he shared with Mary and his mother.

"So you did," Kip said. He and Sarah had chosen to join the rest of the family for a grand Christmas celebration at Thorncliff Manor, bringing their triplets with them. The birth had not been an easy one, but the absolute delight with which he and Sarah had welcomed their boy and two girls into the world made Fiona anxious for her own delivery, which was expected to take place in another couple of months. Frowning, Kip asked his brother, "Did we make a wager?"

"No," Richard replied, "unfortunately not."

"So even you were certain we would marry?" Fiona asked. After all this time, she still could not believe how easily her entire family had seen what she and Edward had failed to realize – that they were perfect for each other.

A bit of easy laughter prompted Fiona to look at her sisters, who were all joined by their husbands on a selection of chairs. "It was an inevitability," Chloe said with a smile. She appeared to be as amused by Fiona's question as Laura, Emily, and Rachel were. "I'm sorry I wasn't here to witness the moment when the two of you finally came to your senses."

"Nobody was there to witness *that*." Lady Duncaster winked and leaned back in a comfy armchair.

The comment produced a blush in Fiona's cheeks. She dropped her gaze, biting her lip the moment she spotted her rounded belly. Looking up from beneath her lashes, she met the warmth of her husband's gaze.

"And that is just as well," he said. He reached for her hand and squeezed her fingers lovingly between his own.

"So tell me, Rachel," Lord Oakland said from where he stood by the fireplace, "how are your scientific pursuits coming along?"

"Quite well," Rachel said, a note of hesitance tingeing her words. Looking at Belgrave, the two appeared to share a secretive smile for a long second before she shifted her gaze to the rest of the family. "Belgrave and I will be traveling to Paris in the spring so I may meet Marie-Sophie Germain. She won a prize from the Paris Academy of Sciences in 1816 for her paper on elasticity theory. As you can imagine, she faced a great deal of opposition on account of her sex but was still acknowledged for her efforts, even though she dropped her male pseudonym and entered the contest as herself. It is my hope to learn from her experience and apply it to my own pursuit of entry in the Royal Academy." She paused and looked toward Belgrave once more before adding, "But as far as my electric lamp is concerned, I have chosen to put it on hold for now since I'll soon be embarking on a close study of children."

A hush filled the room, and then Lady Oakland gasped. "Does that mean? Rachel, are you…"

"Yes, Mama." Rachel's smile was broad and filled with delight as she reached for her husband's hand. "You and Papa will soon become grandparents again."

Loud congratulations followed, along with embraces and handshakes. When it was all over and she was back in her seat, Fiona considered the people who were closest to her heart. It had been a busy year for all of them. It wasn't just Sarah who'd become a mother. Chloe and Mary had both delivered girls one week apart, while Laura and Emily had given their husbands a couple of healthy heirs. The art exhibit and auction Montsmouth had organized for his wife had been written about by critics so favorably, it had turned Emily into an overnight sensation. Her work was now on tour somewhere in Italy, while Laura's latest novel was being read by Mary Shelley, who'd personally requested a signed copy of *The Lady and the Duke*.

A knock sounded at the door and the butler, Caine, stepped in. "My lady," he said, addressing Lady Duncaster. "The nannies have brought all the children to the Christmas room and await your presence there."

"Thank you," Lady Duncaster said. She rose with Lord Oakland's help. "Well, we'd better go join them. I'm sure your nieces are especially eager to unwrap their gifts, Lamont."

"More so than the babies, I'd wager." Lamont followed Lady Duncaster from the room with Laura by his side.

Edward offered Fiona his hand. "Only Lady Duncaster would think to create a Christmas room."

"I love the idea," Fiona said as she let him help her up. Linking her arm with his, she said, "Considering all of her other themed salons, I'm surprised it took her so long to consider it. I dare say it will be a hit with the children who come to visit Thorncliff this summer. Imagine how delighted they will be to celebrate Christmas each day!"

"As delighted as I am to celebrate it with you for the rest of my life, I'll wager."

Tugging his arm, she drew him to a halt, not caring if anyone saw what happened next. She wound her arms around his neck and pulled him down for a kiss. It was gentle and perfect – a loving reminder of how well they suited each other and of how lucky they'd been to stand beneath a bit of mistletoe the previous year.

Acknowledgments

I WOULD LIKE TO THANK THE Killion Group for their incredible help with the cover art and edits. And to my wonderful beta-readers, Carol Bisig, Barbara Rogers, Jacqueline Ang and Barb Hoffarth, thank you for your insight and advice. You made this story shine!

ABOUT THE AUTHOR

Born in Denmark, Sophie has spent her youth traveling with her parents to wonderful places around the world. She's lived in five different countries, on three different continents, has studied design in Paris and New York and has a bachelor's degree from Parson's School of design. But most impressive of all - she's been married to the same man three times, in three different countries and in three different dresses. While living in Africa, Sophie turned to her lifelong passion - writing. When she's not busy, dreaming up her next romance novel, Sophie enjoys spending time with her family, swimming, cooking, gardening, watching romantic comedies and, of course, reading. She currently lives on the East Coast.

You can contact her through her website at *www.sophiebarnes.com*

Or stay in touch with her via the following social media links:

Facebook
Twitter
Goodreads

Pinterest
Instagram

Follow her on Amazon and Bookbub to receive new release updates for her books.

And Please consider leaving a review for this book.

Every review is greatly appreciated!

OTHER BOOKS IN THIS SERIES

Lady Sarah's Sinful Desires
The Earl's Complete Surrender
His Scandalous Kiss

Printed in Great Britain
by Amazon